FINDING FREEDOM

FINDING FREEDOM

SUSAN KIMMEL

Scotland Press
3583 Scotland Road
Building 70
Scotland, PA 17254

Book ISBN : 978-1-941746-49-3
eBook ISBN : 978-1-941746-50-9

Contents

Prologue

"Son, please come closer. I have something to tell you."

Howard Douglas leaned in over the hospital bed, trying to hear his mother's whispers, expecting her to say some last words of endearment, but instead he heard the words, 'You have a brother.' After that, he wasn't sure he heard anything correctly, even though his mother's voice rose a few octaves as she spoke her last request. "Please find him – cave – new hope." She smiled, mouthed the words I love you, closed her eyes and surrendered her soul.

CHAPTER 1

1955

Helen spent most of the morning packing her few belongings in the shabby, black suitcase. She was stuffing each empty space with as many little toys as she could and she was doing it as quietly as possible. This was the last chance for her and her two-year old son to flee. She heard her husband's disgusting belch as he turned the doorknob, giving her the chance to throw the bag under the bed.

The all too familiar, belligerent tone was once again present in his voice as he barked, "Helen what are you doing in here for so long? You know it's lunch time and you should have my food on the table."

The stench of whiskey was so strong, Helen felt nauseated. She used her foot to push the suitcase a little further under the bed before starting toward the door. "I'm sorry, I'll go right now. It will only take me a minute." She flinched as she rushed passed him, hoping to escape another blow to her head. His last punch had sent her staggering. For days, she had experienced blurred vision and headaches. But when she woke this morning, things were clearer and she knew this was going to be the day she would claim her independence.

Helen hummed as she crushed the pill into powder and sprinkled it over the melted cheese on her husband's sandwich. It was just enough to make him sleep for a few hours, giving her time to get away. She thought about crushing a few more, to make it a lethal dose, but he wasn't worth the jail time it might cost her.

Another belch came from his mouth as he motioned for her to come near. With eyes shut, Helen leaned over and allowed his disgusting lips to touch her cheek.

"Pretty good sandwich, woman. When you do everything I tell you, life is good, huh?"

Helen's expression grew hard and resentful as she smiled and answered, "Yes, dear. I'm glad you enjoyed your sandwich. I gave it my special touch."

Helen encouraged her husband to have a drink and enjoy some TV. Before long he was sound asleep on the couch. She emptied the cash from his pockets and took a supply of blank checks from the desk. She retrieved her suitcase and woke her son from his nap. A taxi took her to the bus station and she asked how far she and her son could go on twenty-five dollars. One hundred miles from her husband wasn't all that far, but for Helen, it was enough distance to find freedom for a new beginning.

She rented a one-room cabin and filed for divorce as soon as she was settled. The freedom from living in fear was wonderful, but she was now faced with another problem. The money she had taken was just about gone and she was faced with a difficult decision -- how to continue feeding her son. She had learned to go without food for long periods of time but her son needed nourishment. When Helen kept finding excuses for not paying the rent, the landlord forced them onto the street and for months, a local shelter had become their home. She wanted more for her son than a life of sleeping on cots and eating soup. Her heart broke every night as she listened to her son cry himself to sleep with hunger pains. It became more than she could bear.

Pastor Mike, the visiting pastor for the shelter, recommended a local adoption agency to Helen. She stained the forms with her tears, but she knew it was the only decision she could consciously make. She said goodbye to the most precious gift she had ever been given and tried to never look back.

CHAPTER 2

"And over all these virtues put on love, which binds them all together in perfect unity."

~ Colossians 3:14

1957

Helen soon learned there was so much more to life than loneliness. She missed her son but knowing that *he* was being loved, gave her a peace about her decision. It was the only way she could truly provide for him. Months passed before she heard about a bar, within walking distance of the shelter, where she might find employment. It was time to move on with her own life and to do that she needed a job.

The Cave was a popular tavern that predominantly served seedy clientele. It had been constructed so that the back wall was actually the side of a mountain that contained an entrance to a cave. Strong rumors suggested that it had been a hideout for runaway slaves, but no one ever proved it. As far as anyone could tell, the mountain functioned as a wine cellar.

The owner, Hank Douglas, had been intrigued with the stories surrounding the run-down building and with money he received from his father's estate, he'd purchased the property. Word soon got around, especially among the women, that the new owner was single and easy on the eyes. Before long, the place became a routine stop for the residents. Unfortunately, the establishment also was near the railroad tracks on the industrial side of town. That compromised not only its tangible value, but its social significance as well.

The dimly lit hang-out attracted factory workers and railroad laborers more so than the white-collar city-slickers. Occasionally a classy dressed woman would enter the bar, just to get a look at Hank, order a drink and be gone before he could ask her name. The first time Helen stepped inside, she too had wanted to turn and run, but she was desperate for work.

She had come into the bar as a last resort, but forever grateful that Hank had hired her on the spot. Ironically, she found herself once again spending hours every day serving men who were drunk. But it was different here than when she was married. For one thing, she got paid, and another, Hank never allowed anyone to get aggressive with her. For this reason, she became very loyal. At times, she was afraid of his temper and, crazy as it sounded, she knew she was falling in love with him. She had never seen a more handsome face. It was a mystery to her why he preferred the inside of a dark building when she was sure he could be sitting in a corner office with windows. He kept immaculate bookkeeping journals, ordered his own supplies, resolved his own maintenance issues and, except for a few spills now and then, he made sure the place was spotless. She had seen his framed degree on the wall, selfishly wishing it were hers. She had tried so hard to pursue a degree in business but the unexpected pregnancy had shattered those dreams. With no support from her family, she married the baby's father.

She felt very fortunate to be working for Hank. The longer she worked for him, the deeper in love she fell. He had a heart of gold and had shown sincere kindness when she'd needed it most. He even helped procure her divorce. Sometimes she got the feeling he was falling in love with her, too, but then his mood would change and she would fear him.

"Helen! I got customers out her waitin' for their beers. Where are you? You got two minutes or you're fired!" Helen was probably the only one who heard the words through the roaring din and she was never sure if Hank really meant it or not.

She had learned early on that Hank reacted better when her sentences were similar each time she spoke. If she stayed calm during his outbursts and said, "Comin' Hank," it somehow pacified him. He usually had the temperament of an unfed grizzly but everyone knew underneath his rough exterior he was more like a cub. His regular customers had come to expect nothing less and it gave them incredible leverage with him. His striking good looks totally captured womens' attention, made them more tolerant of his insolence and brought them back time after time. Helen was quite aware of his moods. She probably knew him better than anyone else, and even though he was a bit prickly, she reserved him a place in her heart.

Helen didn't remember exactly how it happened, except that Hank had been in an exceptionally good mood all day and had actually paid her some rather nice compliments. She shrugged them off, thinking it was just one of his many moods, but for some reason he seemed more honest about his feelings, causing her to get caught up in an emotional whirlwind. When she woke up the next morning and found herself next to Hank in his king-sized bed, she panicked. What had she done?

"Good mornin' darlin."

Good mornin' darlin'? Who was he talking to? Was there someone else in bed that she couldn't see?

"Helen? Do you hear me? What's wrong?" Hank rolled over to the edge of the bed and pushed himself to a standing position. Not getting a response, he walked around the bed and waited.

Helen looked up, swallowed past the knot of emotion lodged in her throat, her insides twisted by feelings for the man standing in front of her. Hank hesitantly touched his fingertip to the corner of her eye, brushing away the tears. He was silently watching her, his heart racing with anxiety, while he waited for a verbal reaction. When he got none, he turned away from her and left the room.

Helen found him drinking coffee at his kitchen table. Not sure what to say about last night, she poured herself a cup and moved toward him. "I'm sorry, Hank."

"About what?"

"I'm not sure. Maybe about last night?"

"Well that's a hell of an answer. Do you even remember last night?"

"Sort of. I remember having a few drinks and flirting with you. You were being so nice to me. Was that so you could get me into your bed?"

"No." Her tone aroused and infuriated him all at the same time. "You don't get it, do you? You really don't recognize the fact that I'm in love with you?"

Helen looked as thunderstruck as she felt. She gave Hank a sidelong glance of utter disbelief.

"Aw c'mon, don't pretend like you don't know that!"

"And how would I know that? You don't act like a man in love! What do you think you have done to give me that impression?"

Hunching his shoulders, he turned his mind to the nitty-gritty of the argument. She was right. Up until last night, when had he ever treated her as anything other than an employee? "You're right Helen. There have been so many instances I have wanted to say something romantic to you, but every time I opened my mouth, I realized I'd just be making a fool of myself." He looked at her with something fragile in his eyes, as if in intense pain. "You're out of my league, Helen. You're a beautiful young woman and the only way I've kept my feelings about you under control, is because you deserve so much more. I watch you in this hellhole and it amazes me that you come back to work day after day. The men are crude and the women are calculating, but you seduce them into your way of conduct and they abide by the bar's rules without even knowing it. There hasn't been a brawl here since the day I hired you. That's quite an accomplishment, don't you think?"

Hank's heart-to-heart contained an intimacy she never imagined. Why had it taken so long for him to admit his feelings?

Still a bit hung-over, Helen quickly drank the last few drops of coffee, hoping that would instantly clear her head. "So, are you telling me that last night was real and we weren't intimate just because we had a little too much to drink? And now you're telling me that you love me?"

"That's what I'm telling you."

She hesitated, trying to comprehend what she was hearing. A new and unexpected warmth gushed through her, causing her breath to get caught in her lungs. "I don't know what to say."

"Try saying you'll give me a chance."

Without hesitation she answered, "I'll give you a chance."

Hank was a changed man from that day forward and he and Helen were married ten days later. A warm kernel of happiness occupied the center of Helen's being and there seemed to be a dramatic softening within Hank also. When Helen informed him that she was pregnant, his face broke into a smile.

When the baby was born, tears welled in Hank's eyes as he stared down at the child he had helped bring into the world. Helen had gone into labor while working behind the bar and called out for Hank to help. In the calmest voice she had ever heard him use, he asked, "What do you want me to do?"

"Please call 911 and then come down here on the floor with me. I think this baby is going to get here before the ambulance. Can you find me a pillow?"

"Lucky for you, my back was hurting today and I was using this blue one on my chair. Let me put it under you and see if you can get comfortable."

"Hurry, Hank, I need to push! This one wants to see the world."

Hank stroked her hair and whispered soothingly until her shallow gasps evened out. "Are you supposed be pushing so soon? Shouldn't you wait for the medical team?"

"I can't wait Hank. I need to push NOW!"

"I can't believe it Helen. I can see the head. Push! Push one more time. Push hard, Helen! It's a boy! He's a beautiful, perfect little boy!"

Hank had never experienced such joy until the moment he held his son. He couldn't seem to let go of his tiny fingers. He wrapped him in a towel and laid him beside Helen. With tears rolling down Hank's cheeks, he kept repeating, "He's the most beautiful thing I've ever seen."

Helen lay back, closed her eyes and said, "He's not a thing, Hank. He's our son. He's our strong, handsome son!"

Hank's father had been killed in an accident when Hank was a teenager. The aftermath of his death had resulted in Hank's rebellion. He allowed his anger to lead him on the wrong path, resulting in a criminal record. He now wanted his son to follow a different road. Giving the baby his father's name, Howard Douglas, would surely be a good start.

Life was good for the next two years and Howard was growing into a sweet little boy. He was definitely Hank's crowning glory.

Ten days after Christmas, Helen received a phone call from the state police informing her that Hank had just been involved in an accident and was on his way to the hospital. By the time she arrived, he was gone.

Helen closed the bar for three months, hoping it would be enough time to pull herself together, but she couldn't bring herself to perform the necessary duties without Hank by her side. She decided to keep her ownership, give power-of-attorney to the bank and hire a full-time manager. The night before the transition, Helen sneaked into the room filled with liquor and carved her name and Hank's into the stone wall. Beside it she also wrote both her sons' names and birthdates.

Alone once again, she found a small apartment, away from The Cave, big enough for her and Howard. This neighborhood was full of prostitutes and drug dealers and she soon found herself having conversations with the people on the street. Before long, she too was standing on the corner. She was leaving Howard alone at night, with the understanding that a neighbor would check on him. Children's services were soon notified and Howard was removed from her apartment. She would never forget the day in court as she stood before the judge.

"Mrs. Douglas, as a result of abandoning your son, Howard Aaron Douglas, in order for you to obtain drugs, I have no alternative, but to remove him from your home and place him in foster care." Judge Harper continued, "There have been complaints from your neighbors, on a daily basis. Since your husband's death I know it has been difficult trying to raise a son on your own, but you have not made the best choices. You have put your son at risk. I hereby order you to release your son to the custody of social services before five o'clock today." The judge slammed the gavel, stood, and left the courtroom.

Helen was still high from the last snort. It was a good thing, too, or she would not have been able to cope with the judge's decision. Drugs were the only thing that had gotten her through the months and years since her husband's death. The judge said she had made wrong choices, but what did he know about loving someone the way she had loved Hank. Because of it or in spite of it, another little boy just became a number in the state of North Carolina's foster system.

CHAPTER 3

Do not repay evil with evil or insult with insult. On the contrary, repay evil with blessing, because to this you were called so that you may inherit a blessing.

Peter 3:9

1962

Howard was five when he was placed in the first foster home. He soon learned the meaning of abandonment. In this house, no one hugged him or reminded him of how much he was loved. He missed his mother. He withdrew from any kind of "playing" with the other children and even though he was young, he dreamed of escapes.

"Hey Howard the Coward, should we give you a diaper tonight so you won't pee the bed? You have to wash your own sheets you know!" Rowdy sounds of laughter from the other children would follow as Howard hid in the closet. He had bruises everywhere that wasn't visible to a teacher. The older boys knew exactly how to pinch or hit in places covered by his clothes. Many nights he cried himself to sleep, hating his mother for putting him in this position.

Before long, he was considered a flight risk and was taken to a more secure home. He always convinced himself he was in this situation because of his mother. She was the one to blame and he would never forgive her.

As Howard got older, he found it easier to defend himself. He worked out at the school gym, building muscles, ready to fight back. Even though his foster home was filled with children, he became a loner. By the time he was fifteen, he was in and out of juvenile court three times for causing or starting a physical fight. Each time he was released they sent him to a new foster home, hoping to find an environment that would calm his anger. But until someone could tell him what he had done to make his mother angry enough to give him away, he planned to allow his temper to control him wherever he went.

He managed to graduate from high school and, as soon as the ceremony was over, he packed his few belongings and stood with his thumb high in the air along North Carolina's Route 4. Within minutes, he was riding in a big black 18-wheeler across the state. When the big rig pulled into its warehouse destination in Charlotte, Howard thanked the driver and set off searching for a job.

Within minutes, he realized he was in the poor part of town and the probability of finding a job would be scarce. Houses were rundown and most commercial buildings were empty. There were even a few displaced families living in makeshift tents under the bridges. With the little bit of cash, he had previously saved, he purchased a shirt and a pair of black pants at a thrift store. The clothes were clean, and regardless of what they cost, seemed to provide him with an air of confidence. It was time to find a job.

Even though he thought he was prepared for rejection, it was frustrating each time he heard the word "no." After all, he was willing to do just about anything. He was so thankful for the blanket he had bought at the thrift store, for it made sleeping on a park bench much more comfortable. He was nudged awake by a man in a suit who asked if he could use a little cash. Howard lifted his head and opened his eyes with a critical squint. Did he just hear someone offer him an opportunity to make some money?

A tall dark-clad stranger stood in front of him with a thick crop of nut-brown, unruly hair. The stately figure reminded Howard of a towering spruce in an open field. It was a bit daunting to have the man stand so close to the bench.

Howard spoke with caution, spacing his words evenly. "Excuse me sir, but do I know you?"

The stranger's voice, though quiet, had an ominous quality. "No son, I'm sure you don't, but if you are sleeping on a park bench, using your backpack for a pillow, then I must assume you're homeless and could use a job. Am I right?"

The intensity of the man's gaze seemed to suck the air right out of Howard's lungs and it took him a few seconds before he could speak. When he did, the insecurity in his voice sounded harsh and demanding. "What makes you think I'm homeless? I just lay down here to take a short nap."

"Sure, you did. To tell the truth, I heard your stomach rumbling as I walked by and that usually means it's asking for food. When was the last time you ate?"

Howard wasn't really sure, so he just shrugged his shoulders, wondering exactly why this stranger was interested.

"If you'll walk with me to the diner, I'll buy you some lunch."

As Howard nervously raked a hand through his hair, he asked "Why would you do that? What do you want from me?"

The stranger spit out a wad of tobacco and wiped his mouth. "I'm sorry if I've offended you. I was just trying to do a good deed and offer you a job. We can talk about it over lunch if you'd like."

Howard, still a bit suspicious, but hearing his stomach growl even louder this time, decided that satisfying his hunger pains would enhance his thinking. After all, what was there to be afraid of? It was only lunch and they would be in a public place with lots of other people. He was curious to find out exactly what this dude was all about.

They walked to the only restaurant in sight, a small run-down diner named 'One Man and a Griddle'. As Howard opened the door, the smells wafted out -- smells of cigarette smoke and burnt eggs. Swallowing hard, he fought the urge to throw up, and pressed his hands against his stomach, as if that would help.

The stranger, seeing the color drain from Howard's face asked, "Do you feel all right?"

Howard groaned, and nodded his head. "My stomach has been a bit out of whack the past couple of days and this place doesn't smell all that great.'

"We can go somewhere else if you'd like."

"No, this looks like the only place around, so let's sit down. I just hope the quality of the food is better than the quality of air. It said on the chalkboard outside that today's lunch special is a double cheeseburger, unlimited fries and a chocolate shake. Is it okay if I order that?" He gave a half smile and added, "Those are my three favorite foods."

"You may order whatever you like."

Waiting for the food made Howard uneasy. He played with the silverware and twisted the napkin. He was intimidated by this stranger, who didn't seem to have a need to talk, and it gave Howard the willies.

When the waitress came with the food, Howard began devouring it. The stranger, still silent, seemed to be waiting for just the right moment to speak. While waiting for the next order of fries, Howard asked, "Why are you offering me a job and what do you want with me? I don't even know your name."

"My name is Kingsley Spencer. My friends call me King." He rolled his broad shoulders and leaned back in his chair as if he intended to be awhile. Howard took the opportunity to ask more questions, all the while studying the man. His eyes were the same nutty brown color as his hair and his eyebrows were so out of control that Howard wanted to find a pair of scissors and give them a major trim. His face had a few days' growth of beard and his lips were chapped as if they had endured a lot of sun.

King crossed his arms across his chest and asked," So do you want the job or not?"

"I'm sorry sir, I wasn't listening. What kind of job is it?"

A bit agitated, King tugged at his shirt collar and repeated, "I'm looking for an assistant."

"What does an assistant do?"

King let out a sigh and echoed his earlier comments. "First of all, an assistant listens to his boss the first time, and he does what he is told."

Howard gave a lopsided grin and said, "I'm not really good at that."

"If you take the job, I will teach you. I'll also pay you twenty dollars an hour."

For the first time in many years, hope fluttered inside Howard. Maybe this *is* my lucky day, he thought. I'm broke and I have nowhere to go. Where else am I going to make that kind of money? So, without hesitation, he held out an open hand and felt the strong, steady grip of Kingsley Spencer, his new employer.

CHAPTER 4

For the Son of Man came to seek and to save the lost.

Luke 19:10

1985

"Son, please come closer. I have something to tell you."

Howard Douglas leaned in over the hospital bed, trying to hear his mother's whispers, expecting her to say some last words of endearment, but instead he heard the words, 'You have a brother.' After that, he wasn't sure he heard anything correctly, even though his mother's voice rose a few octaves as she spoke her last request. "Please find him – cave – new hope." She smiled, mouthed the words I love you, closed her eyes and surrendered her soul.

Outside her room, Howard was overwhelmed with this little bit of information. He wasn't sure how the police tracked him down, but learning about his mother's terminal illness had sent shock waves of memories to his heart, forcing him to appear at her bedside.

He knew she had once been a loving mother, always hugging him and reading books. He couldn't remember titles, but he could still picture his bedroom with lots of shelves, filled with books. He remembered tiny toy cars too. All colors, lined up perfectly on those wooden shelves. He hadn't thought of these things in years and now, seeing his mother on her death bed brought back all those memories *and* questions. If he could be found *now*, why didn't she find him before? Had she never looked for him?

Leaving his mother's body in the hospital, was more traumatic than he ever would have imagined. Tears of guilt blurred his vision as he walked out of her room. He wondered why he felt that way. It wasn't like he had any strong family ties, but after all she *was* his mother and silently he *had* promised to find his brother. Brother – the word sounded strange on his tongue yet it brought a smile to his face. What would it feel like to have a brother? Did they look alike? How was he ever going to find him? What if he *couldn't* find him?

With so many questions invading his thoughts, he needed a place to sit down and ponder. He laughed to himself as he recalled sitting on another bench, so long ago, trying to make a decision involving Kingsley. In his heart, he knew he was going to do all he could to find his brother, but what about Kingsley? If he continued his present employment, he would have no time to search for his brother but he knew King would never willingly let him go. He wanted a family; he *needed* a family, and just because he had accepted King's definition of family did not mean he wanted that for the rest of his life.

Howard found himself being consumed with images of a family reunion. Allegiance to Kingsley, for the past ten years, was beginning to be more and more overshadowed with visions of blood. Blood that was just like his, running through veins that could prove he was still part of a real family, not a family made up of gangsters. His twenty-eighth birthday had come and gone while he sat alone in a diner eating scrambled eggs, confirming his thoughts about having no blood relatives to call family. He was beginning to feel as if he too were disappearing. But now, having a real live brother might just change his whole world. Putting so much trust into his mother's disclosure caused him to question his current lifestyle. What was more important, continuing his rogue existence or finding his real family? Without a doubt, he knew the answer to these questions, but how was he going to get away from Kingsley?

Kingsley had taught him how to survive in the world of gambling, but in a family atmosphere, he had no clue. He had been taught how to cheat without getting caught. His natural ability to retain numbers had made him one of Kingsley's key players in casinos around the world. One thing he had learned, a bit late, was that gambling had a way of stripping you bare of, not only your dignity, but all your possessions as well. He got caught up in the embellishments of posh living and found himself immersed deeply in debt. King had promised to make the liabilities go away in return for Howard's eternal, undivided attention to his work. Howard had agreed without hesitation, settling for King's make-believe family.

Was it wrong to want genuine love instead of trying to satisfy your desires with benign respect? Somewhere out there, he had a brother and a chance to be part of a real family. He had promised his mother, and his heart was demanding him to begin the search. His head was reeling with images of his brother. Thinking of them both, brought him to a decision, that in more ways than one, was going to change his life forever. He just didn't know it yet. With no more hesitation, he got up from the bench and walked in the opposite direction of Kingsley Spencer.

CHAPTER 5

For through wise counsel you will wage your war,
and victory lies in an abundance of advisors.

Proverbs 24:6

1988

Clouds of yellow dust drifted from under the cottonwoods as Harley Davidson walked down his usual path to the shed, planning to roll out the water hoses and connect them once again to the spigots. Spring time generated a lot of work outside of Summer Rain Inn, but it was a fair trade-off just to be able to work among the beauty of the blossoms and the fragrances. The gray bones of the trees were beginning to show new life and their tops stirred with the whisper of a morning breeze that sent the sweet smell of lilac and mountain laurel drifting by his nose. He closed his eyes and inhaled, dragging the scent deep into his lungs. He had been right about the ambiance here at Summer Rain. It was abundantly idyllic and brought healing to one's soul. As he looked at the newly-blossoming medley of spring flowers and the huge trunks of deep rooted oak trees, they reminded him of Abby, the owner of Summer Rain, and Mrs. Black, the former owner and mentor of everyone at the Inn – a successful blending of young and old.

He was a paid employee here at the Inn, but he would work for free if it meant being close to Abby. His primary vocation was pastoring the Morning Sun Bible Church in New Hope, but his flexible hours at the church allowed him to also work outdoors, among God's creation, here at Summer Rain.

As he neared the shed, a flash of color, on the ground, caught his eye and he realized it was a red t-shirt. The tag was visible as he bent down to retrieve it. "Men's large," he said outloud. It was clean, folded and infused with a rich smell of cologne. It looked like someone took it from a suitcase and neatly placed it on the ground. But who would be hanging around the garden shed with luggage? The small outbuilding was concealed from Summer Rain's guests by a row of cedar trees that acted as a wall.

He suddenly felt someone watching him, but when he looked over his shoulder, no one was there. He stood still for a moment, listening, but hearing no sounds except the birds, he walked towards the house. He would place the shirt in the lost and found box. Returning to the shed, he still couldn't shake the feeling of being watched. He finished unwrapping the hoses and stepped outside. He heard what he thought was the snapping of a twig. Standing still, he was sure he saw a figure dart behind a tree. He pretended not to notice and casually walked around the backside of the shed and then sprinted towards the tree, ready to pounce! No one was there! Yet, he knew with pulse-pounding certainty that someone was in these woods, and it was making him very uncomfortable. "There it is again, the same crunching sound, like someone walking on dead leaves," he whispered. He stepped behind a tree and waited. He suddenly remembered the small mirror in his pocket, that he'd found on a table on the back patio. He meant to put it in the lost-and-found box but had forgotten all about it until now. He lifted the mirror until he could see in front of the tree. Just then, the breeze shifted and Harley caught a faint scent of the same cologne he smelled on the red t-shirt. Within a few seconds, a baby-faced young man trying to give the impression that he was a range-tough cowboy determined to have his way, stepped out from behind a giant oak tree. Not wanting to alarm the young man, Harley slowly stepped out into the open and, even though he tried to maintain complete control, his voice sounded threatening. "Are you looking for something? Like, maybe a red t-shirt?"

The young man stopped and stood with his legs apart in a warrior's stance, ready to defend his kingdom. He finally spoke with an edge of desperation in his voice, "I'm sorry to be sneaking around like this but what I am looking for will probably sound a bit strange. So, I just wanted to look around a little before I started to ask questions."

"Well, you might want to reverse that. I would appreciate at least being given the chance to answer. What exactly are you looking for, and why here?"

"A cave. I'm looking for a cave."

Harley kept his face hard and unyielding. "Now that's one I never heard before. Looking for a cave. What makes you think there is a cave around here?" Harley gave the young man a half smile, as he asked sarcastically. "Are you looking for some treasure buried by pirates?"

Howard knew this man had every right to make fun of him. He was on the last stretch of his search and if he couldn't find the cave here, he would probably never find his brother. It had now become more than just granting his mother's wish. Finding his brother would be like the beginning of a new identity.

"No sir, no buried treasure such as gold, but if I find what I'm looking for, it will be worth more than all the gold in the world."

"Wow, sounds like it's something pretty important," Harley said.

"It's not some *thing*, it's some *one*. I have recently found out that I have a brother."

Startled by the young man's confession, Harley took a quick breath and apologized. "I'm sorry. I didn't mean to sound so condescending, but why are you looking for your brother in a cave?"

"Well, I'm not actually looking for *him* in the cave but some information that will lead me to him. I have been looking for quite some time now, ever since my mother told me I have a brother. I don't even know his name."

Harley stepped forward and extended his hand. Instinct told him that this young man was as anxious as a child who had stumbled upon something he didn't understand. And rightly so. *If I were in this man's position I would also be doing everything I could to find my brother.*

The stranger shifted his lit cigarette to his left hand and reached out to offer a handshake.

Suddenly a beam of sunlight came streaming through the tree branches, touching the two male hands, as if purposefully thawing the coolness that filled the air. Harley wanted to recognize it as a sign from God, but the young man seemed oblivious to anything out of the ordinary. He stepped back, looking at Harley as if seeing him for the first time, and identified himself as Howard Douglas.

Harley stuck out his hand, "Pleased to meet you. Maybe we could discuss all of this over a cup of coffee. You have peaked my curiosity now about this cave." He motioned Howard to follow him into Summer Rain.

As they entered the kitchen, Shirley was in the process of brewing a new pot of coffee. "Just in time, fellas. Pull up a chair and sit a spell. Nothing like a fresh cup of caffeine. Who's your friend, Harley? New parishioner?" she asked, looking at Howard.

"No Shirley, this is Howard Douglas. He's looking for a cave that holds some very important information about a brother he has never met. Have you ever known any caves to be in this area?"

"No, can't say that I have. What exactly are you looking for?"

"My mother died almost a year ago and on her death bed she told me I have a brother. She whispered--- cave, new hope--- and took her last breath. After I got over the shock of having a brother, I began searching. This is the last town named New Hope that I can find on the map, if that's what she meant, and I'm running out of ideas."

Mrs. Black, looking quite elegant in her peach silk handknit sweater and gray linen pants, leaned toward Howard in her gentle, inquiring fashion and asked, "What was your mother's name?"

"Helen Davis."

"I don't recognize the name and I pride myself on knowing everyone in the area. When would she have lived around here?"

"I don't know. The only thing I'm sure of is that my brother has to be older than I am. I was born in 1957 so it has to be before that."

"Well, my husband and I didn't buy this place until 1962 so she could have lived near here before we moved in. I'll do some checking with some of my 'older' friends and see if they remember anything." Her gentle laugh rippled through the air as she declared, "Most of them can't remember yesterday but I'll get the word around."

The glow of Shirley's smile warmed Harley as he mischievously cautioned Howard about allowing her to get involved in his everyday life. Howard nodded, understanding the look of devilment in Harley's eyes. "Before you know it, this woman will know everything about you, and she'll have you wrapped around her little finger, doing exactly what she wants you to do."

Howard, enjoying this light-hearted bantering, said "Oh no. I don't take orders from women!"

Shirley pressed her hand over her face pretending to be upset at both men's statements, but she couldn't help enjoying the gentle sparring between them and flashed an even more intense Cheshire cat smile.

It was then Howard realized the woman he was bantering with may be what some would call 'old', but she still had a fawnlike beauty. Her skin looked porcelain smooth against her thick, dark hair. Lengthy earrings dangled from her ears. She was a small woman with skinny blue-veined legs. He didn't know much about that sort of thing, but he had to assume she was not in pain, considering all the work Harley had given her credit for. She seemed to have a lot of energy for a woman her age.

Harley, still smiling, but trying his best to look serious, spoke this time, from the heart. "Trust me Howard, if this woman gives you any kind of advice, take it. It's true. Hang around here, and Shirley will have you eating out of her hand." He pointed his finger at Howard and quietly suggested, "If you know what's good for you, you'll take all her advice and memorize it."

Shirley Black dismissed Harley with an abrupt wave and turned toward Howard, peering into his face as though she were studying a painting in a museum. "Where are you staying tonight, young man?"

With the practiced eye of a man who made a living on quick evaluations, he was already in love with this lady. She seemed to be the kind of woman he used to dream about for a mother. There was an energy, an air of enjoying life about her that seemed to exude her very being. "I'm not exactly sure. I figured I would get a room in town."

"Nonsense. You'll stay right here. The Lincoln room is empty right now, ready for a guest. Unless we get super busy you're welcome to stay as long as you need. Where's your luggage?"

Howard wasn't exactly sure how to answer her. He had left his few belongings in a backpack behind the garden shed and it was a little embarrassing to tell this to Mrs. Black. Instead, he mumbled a mostly true fact, "I've been travelling very light since I've been on this mission. I find it's easier that way." The real truth was, everything he owned happened to be stuffed in that ratty backpack.

"Young man. Hello, I'm trying to find out if you want one sugar or two." Mrs. Black, holding a bright blue mug filled with her special blend of coffee, was on the verge of shouting, attempting to get his attention. Even the volume of her voice didn't seem to be enough to bring him back.

Howard heard Mrs. Black talking, but he was obviously having trouble answering her. It was surreal to him that he was standing in front of this gentle woman who was treating him as if he were her long-lost son, wanting nothing from him except to know how he wanted his cup of coffee.

Mrs. Black began waving her arms in front of him saying, "Hello is anyone in there?"

Howard sighed with exasperation and gave a short, embarrassed laugh. "I'm sorry Mrs. Black, I'm a little short on sleep and obviously I need to work on my attention skills. To answer your question, I will have two sugars."

Mrs. Black smiled and passed the cup to Howard as she walked towards the stairs. With a wave of her hand, she gestured for him to follow.

While climbing the stairs, Shirley launched into her own translation of the Civil War, surprising Howard with her knowledge. When she opened the door to the Lincoln Room, Howard was taken aback when he saw Shirley's huge collection and passion for times past. He had never paid a lot of attention to the details in history class but he knew enough to recognize the gray and blue uniforms displayed under glass. Paintings of Lincoln hung on every wall, surrounded by reproductions of plates and cups of that time period. The room was clean, with items precisely placed similar to a museum gallery. Even though it overflowed with historical objects, it still seemed to project an atmosphere of family living.

Howard collapsed into the bed and within minutes was sound asleep.

CHAPTER 6

Do your best to present yourself to God as one approved, a worker who has no need to be ashamed, rightly handling the word of truth.

2 Timothy 2:15

Abby walked into the kitchen wearing a pale yellow shirt and a blazer trimmed in blue leather. Simply put, she was a startlingly attractive woman and Harley still couldn't get used to the idea that he was an important part of her life. Since the first day he met her, she had captivated him.

"You're looking at me as if something is wrong. Do I have food on my face?" Abby said.

"I could never look at you and think something was wrong. Every time I see you, especially here, I have to convince myself all over again that you are part of my life and I really belong here." He smiled as he said, "I was just thinking about the first time we met."

"Harley Davidson, why do you like to remember that day? It's very embarrassing for both of us, don't you think?"

"You might be embarrassed, but I find it somewhat amusing. I'll admit, I was quite rude to you that day when I mistook passion in your eyes for pity. I didn't recognize the difference 'til after you drove away and then I was too ashamed of myself to find you and apologize. The next time I saw you was through the window at the diner and I pretended not to know who you were." Harley's recollection of those early days brought a smile to Abby's face as he continued, "I'll never forget the look on your face the day I showed up at the front door of Summer Rain."

"If I remember correctly, Harley Davidson, when you saw *me* you almost passed out."

Ginning mischievously, he answered, "It was quite the shock to see you open that door. I was expecting Mrs. Black."

Abby crossed her arms and raised an amused eyebrow, "I find it so amazing how God works his wonders in this world. Don't you? We didn't really like each other at first but God had other plans for both of us. Look at us today." Abby planted a kiss on Harley's cheek and walked towards the door.

Harley sighed, and said, "Just so you know, you look beautiful today. Where ya headed?"

"I have a few errands to take care of and then I'm going to the library and ask about local history in this area. Hearing about a cave near this property has me intrigued. Aren't you the least bit interested?"

"As you know, I'm not the adventurous type. I figure Howard came here to search so that's exactly what I'm going to let him do. If he asks for my help, I'll be glad to lend him a hand but otherwise I'm just going to stick to my own schedule. I still have Sunday's sermon to finish and I want to get started with the mowing," Harley replied. He stood watching her, captivated by her southern-belle charm. "Don't get yourself so caught up in this little cryptic venture. How do we even know he's telling the truth?"

"We don't, but where's your faith, Harley? I think God sent him here. I don't know why, but remember what we were just talking about? If I hadn't taken a leap of faith when I bought the Inn, you and I would not be together. You *do* believe that was God's doing, don't you?"

The sort of smile that forces one to grin back at it came across Harley's face. "That's why you are so good for me Abby, you have a way of reminding me of my purpose here on earth. I do believe God put you in my path. I'm not sure where I would be if it weren't for you and Shirley."

"Well, let's just be thankful we followed God's plan and let's have faith again that Howard was sent here for a reason. I just have this feeling knowing him is going to change our lives somehow." Abby placed her hand on Harley's forearm, gave him another quick kiss on the cheek and hurried out the door. He had that same feeling too. He just wasn't sure he was ready for it.

Harley walked to the garden shed and unlocked the door, excited to remove the tarp from the mower and hear the roar of the engine. It was officially the first day of spring, which meant warmer temperatures, allowing him to spend time with God in this place of solitude. As soon as he was done mowing he would find refuge under the shed's weathered roof; where some of his best sermons had been written.

He chuckled as he thought about his comeback debut just months ago, at Morning Son Church. When he stood in front of his congregation feeling confident, yet significantly unworthy, he spoke from the heart and delivered the most passionate life lesson, in the form of a sermon, he ever imagined possible. He still thanked God every day for allowing the right words to flow from his mouth. It definitely was a turning point in his life.

Harley's musings were interrupted by a familiar-sounding male voice. As he turned around, the first thing he noticed was Howard's muscular arms wedged into the red t-shirt. He was rather slim, but powerfully built. His voice seemed equally as strong this morning.

"Hi, Harley. Do you need any help?"

"Thanks, Howard, but I'll be leaving as soon as I get done with the mowing. I have some church obligations to take care of today."

"Church? You the janitor or something?"

This time Harley couldn't keep a straight face, and his smile deepened into laughter. "Is it that obvious that I'm a janitor?"

"Well you're certainly dressed like one, and besides, who else but the janitor has any work to do at a church?"

"Well, believe it or not, Howard, pastors work more than just on Sundays."

Howard's brown eyes widened in realization. "You're a preacher? A real preacher?"

"Well, some might disagree with you, but yes, I'm the pastor at the Morning Son Bible Church in New Hope."

A rush of bitter memories almost overtook Howard's ability to speak. Old feelings and memories flooded him, catching him off guard. He wasn't fond of preachers. He thought of them as human tranquilizers. They always gave you a shot of hope and made you numb to all the bad things in your life. They were masters of persuasion, making you believe God really cared, but when you really needed him, the Almighty was nowhere to be found, and neither were the preachers. Nothing they promised ever came true. He had learned early that it didn't pay to care about anyone or anything.

Now here he was, standing face to face with a real live preacher. Did he have to be nice to him, just because he said he was a 'holy man'? In all seriousness, he actually liked this guy and he didn't seem phony like all the other 'men of God' he had been forced into talking with when he was in the foster care system.

As Harley waited for some kind of reaction to his announcement, he sensed a bit of murkiness within the soul of this young man. The lines of his face were etched with deep concern, causing Harley to wonder just what had happened in Howard's past to cause such a foreboding expression. "Howard, are you all right? You look as if you've seen a ghost."

Trying to act nonchalant, Howard shrugged and said, "I do?"

Harley's smile once again turned to a chuckle as he pointed out, "I've never had anyone actually react to my being a pastor in such a somber way. Is there anything I can do to help?"

"Yeah. Don't start preachin' to me." The words were sudden and raw and very angry.

Waves of grayness passed over Harley as he raised his hands in a don't shoot pose. "Obviously something has happened in your past to cause such ill feelings but I wouldn't think of interfering. Let me say this one time. If you ever need to talk, come find me and I'll listen." He turned and walked away reluctantly, hating himself for not being able to find a way to communicate with this obviously troubled young man.

CHAPTER 7

"Do not judge by appearances, but judge with right judgment."

John 7:24

When the community had judged Harley as a common crook instead of believing in him as their pastor, the anxiety was more than he had ever experienced. It was so unsettling how people chose the dramatic version of a story rather than ask questions and discover the truth. His mother had been strict about hearsay. "Harley, if you have something to say about someone and it isn't good, I don't want to hear it."

Because of the guilty judgment from the church board and the community, Harley was more aware than ever of casting judgment prematurely. But even as a pastor, it was hard not to judge someone like Howard. Harley found it hard to believe or trust him. He had showed up, sneaking around the property, supposedly looking for a cave, and ended up occupying a room at the Inn. Harley just didn't know what to think. The past situation at the church had definitely put his faith to the test, and sadly caused him to look at people differently now.

In spite of his determination to forget those two years of being portrayed as a thief, Harley's mind seemed to revisit those days more often than he wanted. He had to admit, if only to himself, that the past was never far away. In his heart he knew he had truly forgiven everyone for their allegations, yet trying to erase two years of those memories was becoming quite the challenge. Every time he tried to dismantle and separate them from the pleasant ones, he found himself not quite up for the under taking. Even though it had been a frustrating and dismal time in his life, the experience had given him super insight into the world of compassion and forgiveness. In hindsight, he could now say that he was glad he had been given the opportunity to live in the shoes of a homeless person and to know how it feels to be accused of something you didn't do. The real-life experience also gave him a better understanding of humility. It had brought him to his knees on a regular basis.

The unexpected whine of an ambulance siren jolted Harley out of his pensive mood. He had a lot of work to do today, no time for evoking a lot of memories.

"Harley? Harley are you out there?"

At the sound of Abby's shout, Harley stopped and listened. He knew something was terribly wrong. As he reached the back patio, Abby was leaning against a table looking as if she were ready to pass out. The minute she saw Harley she burst into tears. "Come quick – it's Shirley. The ambulance is almost here."

"What happened, Abby? Did she fall?"

"I think it might be her heart. Hurry Harley, she's in the kitchen."

Seeing Shirley on the floor created a sudden chill to run through Harley's body. He had never seen this woman so still. She was still breathing but it was slow and erratic. Just as he knelt down beside her, the paramedic was looming over him, asking him to please move out of the way.

Harley and Abby stood back and watched helplessly as the two medical responders quickly positioned the oxygen mask on Shirley's face and then proceeded to run an Electrocardiogram for determining whether it was a heart attack. The test proved them to be right and within minutes she was laid on a gurney and the ambulance whisked her away to the hospital.

Abby began crying, unable to control her tears. Her trembling arms clung tightly to Harley as she pleaded, "Harley we have to get to the hospital right now. Hurry Harley."

Driving faster than he had ever driven before, Harley managed to reach the hospital parking lot and slid into a space near the emergency room. Abby was out the door before the car came to a complete stop. By the time she reached the waiting room, she was out of breath and crying so hard, the nurse had to wait for Harley just to find out why they were there.

Once inside the little room where they wheeled Shirley, Abby broke down and cried yet again. The woman she called 'Mom' was barely visible underneath a mass of machines and tubes. She lay as motionless as a wax statue.

Abby tried to listen carefully as the doctor confirmed it was a heart attack. There had been substantial damage to Shirley's heart but he was optimistic about her recovery. She would probably no longer be able to help with the cooking or cleaning at the Inn, but, with some rest, she should regain most of her strength, able to live out her remaining years comfortably.

Abby drew a deep breath through her nose, worry tightening the delicate features of her face. She swallowed hard, as hot tears slipped down her cheeks. She leaned over the bed and placed a kiss on Shirley's forehead. "Mom, I promise I'll come back to see you soon. Now rest."

CHAPTER 8

For I consider that the sufferings of this present time are not worth comparing with the glory that is to be revealed to us.

Romans 8:18

The ride home to Summer Rain was bittersweet for Abby and Harley. Both were happy Shirley was still alive, but heartbroken that she was so sick.

"Harley, do you think Shirley will be able to come home soon?"

"I'm praying as hard as I can Abby, but you know it's in God's hands at this point."

"I know, but I guess I'm just not ready to handle more grief. It seems like only yesterday that I buried my husband and I'm really not ready to bury someone else that I love dearly." Abby hesitated, then spoke with quiet, but desperate, firmness, "She has to come home, Harley."

Harley wanted to say some reassuring words but none came to mind. He could only imagine the flood of memories that must be floating around in Abby's mind. How painful it must be to recall that fateful day of rushing to the hospital and finding her husband gone from her forever.

This time the outcome was different. Shirley was still alive and expected to recover. He turned to look at Abby and saw her pained expression, as though she'd been wounded, and in all honesty, she had been. A knife to her heart would have given her no less pain.

Harley parked near the front of the Inn, got out, and opened the car door for Abby. He reached for her hand to help her out of the car but she remained frozen in the seat.

"Abby, c'mon let's go into the house. The temperature is dropping and you don't have a sweater."

"I don't want to go in the house." Abby suddenly felt threatened by the vastness of the Inn. She had never walked through the door without Shirley being present somewhere on the grounds. And now, knowing that she wasn't inside, gave her a sense of emptiness. A feeling that she hadn't encountered for some time. From the day Shirley signed ownership of the Inn over to Abby, Shirley stepped in the background and gave Abby full reign of the house; but her presence still permeated every space. She had this incredible way of influencing everyone who came through the front door. Abby especially attributed Joan, their housekeeper's amazing redemption, to Shirley. Without her godly passion for life, the atmosphere at Summer Rain would not exist.

Harley opened the car door and stood patiently waiting for Abby to get out. He saw giant tears rolling down her cheeks as she slowly swung her legs to the ground. She took Harley's hand with no exchange of words, and walked towards the front door. Joan, still wearing her rubber gloves and looking a bit scruffy, was there to greet them as they entered the foyer. She didn't seem to care about her appearance as she pushed back the escaping hair from the all too familiar bandana. She took one look at Abby's eyes, bloodshot from hours of crying, and also broke down in tears.

"How is Miss Shirley? Is she coming home soon?" Joan could hardly get the words out between the sobs but Abby offered a hug; the two women became engaged in their shared anxiety about Shirley.

Harley was thankful that, at times like this, he could rely on God's guidance to provide him with just the right words of comfort. He gently pulled Abby away from Joan and guided her to a chair. He knelt down beside her, but, knowing that pushing her too hard would be a mistake, he waited. He was planning on quoting some scripture but before he even opened his mouth, Abby placed her hand on his forearm and said quietly "I am going to take a shower and I'll be okay." Harley nodded in agreement and turned toward the kitchen, hoping Joan had made some coffee.

The penetrating ring of the hall phone generated immediate fear in Harley as he picked up the receiver. He took a deep breath, quickly changing his sad expression into one of happiness. "Abby is getting some rest but I will give her the message. Thank you." He exhaled a long breath of relief. Shirley was going to be okay! The nurse who called from the hospital didn't know exactly when she would be able to come home but she *would* be coming home!

Exhaustion took over and Abby almost melted into her pillow. She didn't remember it ever feeling so inviting. But rest didn't come as easy as she thought it would. Images of Shirley being whisked away in the ambulance kept getting in the way of her sleep. Harley quietly opened Abby's bedroom door and whispered, "Abby, are you awake? I need to talk to you."

Abby rolled over quickly, facing him, fearing the news was not good. Harley, even though he always seemed to bear what part of the burden he could, was showing no real signs of panic. Nonetheless, she wrapped her arms around her pillow like a child holding a favorite doll, cast her eyes downward, and expected the worst.

"Shirley is awake and waiting to talk to you."

With a springy bounce, Abby was off the bed executing a playful pirouette and before Harley knew what was happening, he was taking her full weight as she flew into his arms. "Really Harley? That's wonderful news. What are we waiting for? Let's go!" She had already taken three steps in one movement and was running to the car on the same momentum. Harley had no choice but to follow her.

Once again, Harley barely had the car in the parking space before Abby had the door open and focused on finding the elevator out of the parking garage. Not waiting for him, she pushed the 'down' button and was gone. Harley smiled as he watched her disappear behind the elevator doors. He had never seen her as excited or happy.

Even though the bed was elevated to a sitting position, Shirley was clearly sound asleep. A half-eaten bowl of green jello sat on the bed tray, indicating that Shirley fell asleep while in the middle of her lunch. The once strong, robust, mite of a woman now looked weak and defeated. Abby stepped back out into the hallway and leaned hard against the wall. How am I ever going to go back in that room and be strong? Strong, like Shirley would want me to be. Determined to prove her strength, she turned, ready to enter the room again when she looked up and saw him standing there, watching her.

"Hi Harley. Sorry I didn't wait for you, but I was just so anxious to talk to Shirley that my instinct was to run. When I walked into the room, she was sleeping so soundly that I didn't have the heart to wake her so I came out here, just to get my bearings before I went back in."

"It's okay, Abby, but *I* feel your pain too. We all would be lost without her." He took her by the hand and they walked silently to Shirley's bedside as Abby lightly touched her shoulder. It took several seconds for Shirley's eyes to adjust to the rooms lighting, but when they adapted, her face showed recognition and she flashed a smile of thanks.

Abby burst into tears, leaned over and kissed her on the top of the head. Shirley reached for Abby's hand and they laced their fingers together. The entire hospital room seemed to be filled with an incredible softness as the two women immersed themselves in each other's presence. Harley dropped a feather light kiss to Abby's cheek as he whispered, "I am going back to the Inn. Please call me when you are ready to come home." She nodded her head to indicate 'yes' and mouthed the words, "Thank you."

Chapter 9

O mountain of Mine in the countryside, I will give over your wealth and all your treasures for booty, Your high places for sin throughout your borders.

Jeremiah 17:3

Howard reached for the cord and drew the blind to cover the window. The heat from the morning sun was intense and the stifling air in his bedroom had already caused him to throw the covers aside. Even though the room was rather large, the bed had been placed directly beside the double window. Even with the blind drawn, he found it impossible to return to sleep. Maybe it was just as well. Sleep was not his friend. It only brought images of dark caves peppered with symbols of religion, gushing forth into a torrential river where he always stood trying to decipher exactly what they meant before they were washed away. Over the roar of the water, a desperate voice, as familiar as his own, called from within the cold walls asking for guidance out of the cave. But his words never seemed to reach the faraway cries. He woke up drenched, as if the ripples of the river had swept him under. He made his bed and was tidying up his bathroom when he heard a knock on his door. When he opened it, Abby anxiously held a cup of coffee out to him. He could tell something was on her mind.

"Well, to what do I owe this pleasure, Miss Abby? I was just about to come downstairs."

"I know, but I couldn't wait any longer. I have some news about a few caves in the area. Do you want to hear?"

"Yes, of course."

"Good, I have everything laid out on the table in the sunroom. See you there in five minutes."

A strange, cold excitement filled Howard's whole being. What if they really did find a cave? And what if they even found some information about his brother inside the cave? Would there be enough clues to locate him or would it just be another wild goose chase? He was tired of searching, yet he was gritty enough to maintain a Sherlock Holmes pursuit and not give up. He had been involved in a lot of shady dealings in his short lifetime, caused a lot of trouble for a lot of folks, but he was still a man of his word. He promised himself he would honor his mother's dying wish and no matter how long it took, he would look for his brother until all possibilities were exhausted. He was hoping to find him and perhaps settle down somewhere nearby. He was tired of his past lifestyle. The velvet trap of easy living and hard drugs had taken its toll. Working for powerful men, who insisted they were not Mafia connected, was an intense day-to-day occupation. Pain and loneliness walked with him wherever he went. He was at the dead end of hopelessness when his mother fell ill, but because of her death, he now had another chance at living. King had given him a few days liberty to go to the hospital, and because he was such a loyal employee for the past ten years, did not feel it necessary to assign a body guard. Howard knew the high stakes of desertion, but his future had been looking vague and shadowy for some time now. This quest he was on - it seemed to be the perfect chance for him to break away from the appalling life that he found himself living.

When he was younger, hunger and desperation had goaded him into crime, eventually producing a perverse pleasure in each assigned challenge. But, finding out that he had a brother inspired new feelings. Would he be able to vanish from King's control, or would he always be competing with shadows of the big man? How long before King's nefarious henchmen would stumble upon his location? If that happened, he would have to move on quickly. King's men would not hesitate to hurt anyone who got in his path and Howard wanted no harm to come to anyone at Summer Rain. As much as he tried not to think of the consequences of his discovery, the thought invaded every space of his heart.

Standing at the top of the stairs, ready to descend to the kitchen where Abby was waiting for him, Howard knew he had about thirty seconds to vacate his previous thoughts. Under the instruction of King, he had spent many hours learning how to recognize body language as a means of deciphering the genuineness about someone or suspecting dishonesty. Almost within minutes he could recognize and identify a person's character. He had immediately decided that Abby and Harley were both the "real deal." However, he also felt that Abby was just as competent as he was, with her sensitive and perceptive approach to issues. She seemed to have a natural ability to sense truth. He smiled as he thought about the last few days. Obviously, he had passed the character test.

Driven by the strong aroma of coffee, he detoured by the kitchen, poured more of the delicious-smelling liquid into his mug and proceeded to the sun room. Spread across the table were books, papers and most importantly, maps. Abby was so engrossed in one of the books that she missed his arrival. She nearly fell out of her chair when he spoke.

She burst out, shocked, "Don't sneak up on me like that!"

"I'm sorry Abby, but you did ask me to come see you. I didn't realize you were so lost in thought."

"It's okay. I seem to be a little jumpy these days. Please sit down and let me show you what I have found."

The two poured over the maps for the next hour, trying to identify the exact location of each cave included in the legend of the map. Each time they discovered what they thought might be the site, it turned out to be on the wrong side of the mountain or too far north.

"Wow, what are you two doing? Looks like you're up to your eyeballs in paperwork."

"Mom! What are you doing out of bed? Remember what the doctor said. You are supposed to be resting."

"I think I've rested enough. Just being home gives me a sense of peace. It's so wonderful to be back in my own bed again." Shirley, leaning hard on her cane, but still carrying herself with vigor and grace, spoke directly to Abby. "I'm going to try some cooking today. I feel very strong and I'm hungry." Abby began to protest, but Shirley held up her hand in a 'stop' gesture and said, "Do not argue with me today. I'm afraid you'll lose." She pointed her cane in the direction of the kitchen, but with a spontaneous movement, she faced Howard and Abby again. She exchanged a wide, sheepish smile with Abby and waited.

"Why are you looking at me like that, Mom? What are you up to?"

"Oh, I just remembered something. Would you like to know what it is?"

"Am I going to like it? Is it something about your health?"

"Oh, I think you both will be happy."

Abby looked at Howard, rolling her eyes, wondering just what this woman was up to.

"Remember when I told you I would ask my 'old' friends if they knew of any caves?"

Abby started jumping up and down. "They know where it is? Why didn't you tell us before this? That's what we were trying to figure out when you came into the room. But we keep running into dead ends."

"Hold on girl, don't get so excited. I do have some information and I hope it will help but I can't be sure if my old friend Mr. Henry's memory is still intact."

Nearly exploding with anticipation, Abby burst out, "Well tell us right now. Is there really a cave near here?"

"According to Mr. Henry there is a cave somewhere at the far corner of our property, near the base of the mountain. He remembers a story his mother used to tell him when he was a young boy. She and her friends used to play in what she called 'a hole in the side of the mountain.' She told him that she used to sneak out of the house with the family flashlight. She wandered into the dark hole and tried to figure out what all the pictures that were carved into the stone walls meant. Mr. Henry remembers his mother telling him this story but she never told him exactly where it was and he and his buddies were never very adventurous." Shirley smiled as she continued. "But he does have an idea where you should look."

Abby jumped up so fast she knocked over the chair. "Did he tell you? Where is it?"

"Yes, he told me and no, I don't know exactly where it is; if you wait a minute I will give you the directions he gave me." Shirley fished a crumpled paper out of her pocket and graciously handed it over to Abby.

"Local historians believe it was used as a shelter for the runaway slaves in the underground railway system."

Before Shirley could continue with more history, Abby interrupted. "Can we go there now? C'mon Howard, get your coat."

"How is it possible that a woman such as yourself, could get so excited about going into an old dark, cold cave? Most women would be petrified," Howard said.

Abby grinned mischievously, "Well, then, I guess you can assume that I'm not most women."

A lazy taunting smile slid from one side of his beard-stubbled jaw to the other before Howard answered. "I've already allowed myself that assumption."

Abby stared at him silently for a minute, words caught in her throat. Not exactly sure how to answer, she decided to dismiss his response and pretend that she had never heard it.

"Howard, would you like to go on an adventure today? I have never actually walked the entire grounds of my property so this gives me a great reason to do so. I'm going to see if Harley can spare some time today and the three of us can go exploring."

A smile and a nod of consent from Howard was all it took for Abby to pick up the phone and dial Harley's number.

CHAPTER 10

"For you shall go out in joy and be led forth in peace; the mountain and the hills before you shall break forth into singing, and all the trees of the field shall clap their hands."

Isaiah 55:12

Harley arrived within the hour and went straight to the shed. Not exactly sure what kind of equipment they might need if they actually found this cave, he took the lantern from the shelf and a garden rake from the wall. This would help remove any overgrowth of bushes. Armed with his tools, he began the walk up the path towards the house. Howard and Abby were patiently waiting for him by the car as he put his tools in the trunk and jumped in behind the wheel. The far north side of the property was farther than any of them wanted to walk, so they had decided to drive as far as the road would allow.

Most of the acreage lay undeveloped at the base of the Humpback Mountain. Seeing the outline of the land on a map seemed good enough for her at the time of settlement. Now as they drove down the dirt road, she realized she had purchased an extraordinary piece of real estate. Shirley never went into detail about the area beyond the manicured gardens and Abby had never really inquired. Working with Shirley to enhance the interior of the Inn had required all her energy and time. She never had a reason to ramble through the woods.

As she exited the car, she was amazed at the beauty that surrounded her. Her mind was already racing, envisioning bike paths and trails for walking. Guests at the Inn would love having this touch of nature as part of their retreat. Somewhere in the distance she heard water gurgling, possibly a stream, hopefully, a small waterfall. She made a quick visual sweep of the vicinity and realized it could be made into a small paradise. Loblolly pines stood tall, their clumps of pine needles gently swaying in the wind. Had she just landed on a different planet? How could she have not even wanted to inspect this wooded portion of her new home.

Why hadn't Shirley ever mentioned this north side of the estate? She had to know it existed. The three soon realized they had unconsciously followed the sound of the water. The earthy scent of wet rocks and decomposing wood filled their nostrils. They came upon a shallow creek and admired its formidable twists and turns. They watched as a small amount of pine needles meandered their way downstream.

Sunshine broke across her face as Abby turned toward Howard, "I want to thank you, for giving us a reason to come here and discover this wonderful spot."

Howard bowed respectfully and smiled, but didn't answer.

Abby aimed her next sentence at Harley. "Look around us. Doesn't this remind you of your willow tree hideaway? It's peaceful, quiet and I think it could be very therapeutic."

Harley smiled with remembered pleasure. The old willow tree served him well. For some reason, it always seemed to have a calming effect on him when he was at his lowest. Resting under the green wispy branches had always seemed to refresh his energy and his perseverance. The church, too, had been his sanctuary, but after his dismissal from his pastoral duties, he'd found refuge under the old willow. It was there he could kneel on the spongy moss and pour out his heart to God.

"Harley, are you listening? Think about this. Our motto for Summer Rain is that we want to help folks find peace with themselves and peace with God. Wouldn't this be the perfect place for people to come and be renewed?"

"I think it would be wonderful."

"We could strategically place some benches in this area. Near the water and maybe deep within the trees, very private. Can you visualize all of this Harley? Do you know how to build a bench?"

"One question at a time, please. You're getting way ahead of yourself. I do think all of this is possible but it won't happen overnight. And, remember why we came out here. We need to spend a little more time looking for this mystery cave and wait until we get back to the inn to talk about your ideas for a forest renovation."

Abby frowned thoughtfully, then burst into an audacious smile. She knew Harley was right but she also knew with quiet assurance that he would make her vision come true. Smiling at him was her way of promising patience.

A hair-raising, thunderous shout caused Abby and Harley to leave their dreamy ideas beside the stream and follow the unnerving commotion. They had only walked twenty yards when Howard came dashing by, followed by a swarm of bees. He was cursing, spitting out words Abby had never heard before, all the while swatting and flailing like a drowning man.

"Run towards the car and get inside as quickly as you can and drive back to the house. We'll meet you there," was all Harley could think to yell. He had never seen anything like this. There must have been fifty yellow jackets following Howard and they seemed to be catching up with him.

The two watched as Howard drove away and then they both doubled over with laughter. It was quite a comical scene even though they knew bee stings could be dangerous; Howard could be allergic. Their only hope was that he made it to the car before getting stung.

As they began their long walk back to the Inn, Harley gently took hold of Abby's hand, slipped it through the crook of his arm and squeezed her to him. Words didn't seem necessary as she rested her head on his shoulder and exhaled a very contented sigh.

As they neared the driveway, they could see Abby's car parked in front of the garage door but Howard was nowhere in sight. Suddenly, their country privacy was being invaded with sounds of bee stinging pain. Howard obviously had no idea that his voice had gone airborne and was now suspended in the still air.

As they entered the kitchen, it was easy to identify the source of the uproar. Shirley was standing over Howard trying to sterilize all the red bumps with some sort of cream. She was pinching her lower lip with her teeth while trying not to make a joke, even while Howard was flinching.

Abby and Harley started talking at the same time, reliving the chase of the bees. When Shirley started humming 'The Flight of the Bumble Bee' even Howard grimaced in good humor. His arms and neck all dotted with white cream, Shirley instructed him to sit still while she went looking for some more medicine. She returned with two tablets and a glass of water. She watched while he swallowed them and then ordered him to bed. As much as he wasn't into taking orders, there was something in Shirley's tone that touched a place inside him. In the past he always rebelled at orders but taking them from this woman was different.

CHAPTER 11

In his hand are the depths of the earth,
and the mountain peaks belong to him.

Psalm 95:4-5

"Howard, do you think you are ready to go back out into the woods?" Abby asked.

"Yeah, it'll take more than a few bee stings to keep me from exploring. But this time let's take some spray to kill those little devils. I think we can get close enough to the nest to spray without getting them so stirred up. Once they're all dead we'll try to hack through that underbrush. It was particularly thick in that area so we'll need to work a little harder with the axe. If old Mr. Henry was right, then we have to keep looking until we find something."

Driving back down the secluded lane brought the return of many ideas and visions to Abby's attention. It was beautiful here and she wanted to share its splendor with her guests. But right now, she had to concentrate on helping Howard find the cave. And, she knew that in due time, Harley would bring her dream to fruition.

Harley stopped the car, and once again everyone piled out, ready for more exploring. Howard went in the opposite direction of the bees' nest while Harley walked directly towards it. The swarm had calmed down considerably and had gone back to their old dead tree hidden behind some very thick elderberry bushes. A few bees were still buzzing around but didn't seem threatened. He decided to explore a thick patch of bushes a little further down from the nest and see if he could find a new way around the thicket. The bushes seemed to be in rows, not natural for wild foliage. He had a gut feeling that someone had planted these bushes hoping to make it look natural, in order to hide something, but the space between the rows was still somewhat visible. He found a few dead bushes, allowing him a small gap in the density of the tangled thicket. He snipped the dead twigs until he could maneuver his body through to the other side. And there it was. A big hole in the side of a stone wall. This had to be the entrance. Before notifying the others, he decided to look a little closer. Some sort of vine had grown near the top but there was still sufficient room for him to wiggle inside. He grabbed his flashlight and shined it towards the ceiling. Just as he figured – hundreds of bats. He immediately stepped backwards and found his way back through the opening in the bush and ran. He was so out of breath when he found Abby and Howard he could barely describe the scene, but he had no problem stating he would not return.

While Abby found his anxieties to be amusing, Howard understood. "How are we going to get inside that cave? I'm not going in and obviously neither are you. Who are we going to find that's brave enough, or crazy enough, to go in a cave filled with real live bats?"

Abby quickly answered, "Let's go back and quiz Shirley."

Sure enough, Shirley gave them the phone number of an exterminator. She wasn't sure if he had ever gotten rid of bats but it was worth a try. The man showed up the next morning and Howard drove him out to the cave. He was in total shock to see the number of bats hanging inside the cave and told Howard that even if he managed to get rid of them, there was no guarantee they wouldn't return. Howard explained the reason for the mission, saying that if they would only stay away for a week, it would be enough time to find a clue.

CHAPTER 12

Many are the plans in a person's heart,
but it is the Lord's purpose that prevails"

Proverbs 19:21.

The purging of the bats proved to be a worthwhile gamble. Howard talked Harley into going with him for the first exploration in the newly-found cave. Full of defensive adrenaline, the two entered the chilling darkness with high powered lanterns. With only one foot inside, they simultaneously pressed the buttons on their lanterns, creating an instant glow and two audible sighs of relief. It was amazing how cold it was without the warmth of light. Nothing fluttered or flew, at least for the moment, but each carried a tennis racket, just in case. Both men strained their ears, listening for noises, but as they moved forward the only sound was the echoing of their footsteps. It took several seconds for their eyes to adjust and the rancid stench of bat droppings abruptly forced them to cover their noses. The floor of the cave was slippery and uneven making it not only scary, but dangerous as well.

"How far do you think we have to go before we see something?"

"I don't know, Harley, but if you want to go back, I'll totally understand."

Harley's senses seemed to lift to the next level when he removed his hand from his nose just long enough to reply. "For some reason, Howard, I feel like my breastplate of armor is on and I'm ready for battle." He blew out his cheeks and said, "Although I must tell you, I'm also fervently praying that we don't come in conflict with creepy, sticky wings."

Howard, not wanting to admit to those same thoughts, waved the tennis racket high in the air and laughed, a kind of trilling laugh of sympathy. "Don't worry preacher man, we'll get 'em."

As they moved further into the cave, the rocks surrounding them appeared more rugged and worn. A ledge ran evenly around the now curved wall, obviously shaped by the many years of being beaten by water. The rhythmic dripping seemed to produce a sort of background harmony with hints of wind as it whistled through the tiny moss-covered crevices. Without warning, the floor of the cave sloped downward, taking them into a whole new chamber filled with stalactites hanging from the ceiling. The lantern's bright beams on the icicle shaped formations transformed them into beautiful prism-like crystals.

"I'm not liking this, Howard. What do you think we're looking for anyhow?"

Howard hesitated for a moment, and then said, "Your guess is as good as mine."

Harley spoke slowly, feeling his way along the rock ledge, "So you're serious? You have no idea what we're even looking for?"

Through the faint beginnings of a smile, Howard replied, "You got it preacher man. I was hoping your God would help us."

The cadence of his voice sent an odd jolt to the pit of Harley's stomach. "*My* God? What do you mean by *my* God?"

"Well, he's sure not mine. What's He ever done for me?"

"Okay, let's address that question. You're here aren't you? Looking for a long-lost brother that you didn't know you have. You got to your mother just in time for her to tell you about him, and you think all this happened just because?"

"And you think God orchestrated all of this?"

"Honestly? Yes, I do. I don't know all the details of your childhood and your recent years but I get the feeling that you're not real proud of them. In God's eyes, the past doesn't really matter. It's your future He cares about. He has a plan for you, for all of us. The only thing we need to do is sit back and trust Him."

Only with the glow of the lantern could Harley see Howard's face taut with interest, ravenously feeding on his words. Did that mean he was passionately listening or was the intensity in his eyes of a malicious nature? Should he continue and hope for a response, or should he just be quiet? Within seconds, Harley got his answer.

"I told you no preachin to me, preacher man. If I have to listen to this all the time, maybe finding my brother isn't worth it after all. But since I'm here, I'm gonna be moving further into this dark hole. If you're comin' then stay close behind me and if you're not comin' then you can stay right where you are or go back outside alone."

"No way man, am I standing here alone. Two lights are better than one."

The pair made their way down what seemed to be a well-worn footpath into the fairly wide chamber giving them both an odd, volatile feeling about the space in front of them. Howard held his lantern at arm's length, high above his head, turning slowly like a merry-go-round, hoping to observe every angle of the dark place. He twisted nearly halfway around when he suddenly stopped, and sucked in a quick breath, like someone about to plunge into icy water. Just about the same time, Harley backed up a hasty half-step.

"What is that?"

"I don't know. It looks like a pile of bones. It's not moving so I'm going to get a little closer." Howard, shoulders slumped and moving at the speed of a slug, finally reached the collection of remains. He groaned, and for a moment stood facing the bones but not looking directly at them. "Who do you think these people were and why would they have been in this cave?"

"Obviously, they didn't come on their own free will. It looks like they huddled together in order to stay warm. Do you think they were lost?"

"Well, I don't think they were here on vacation."

"I guess that was a pretty dumb question."

"Yeah, preacher man, it was. Got any other bright observations?"

"Okay, okay. I've just never seen anything like this. All I can think of are the pictures of the Jews in the concentration camps."

Harley shook his head negatively, trying to envision the poor souls who, for some reason, whether they entered the cave voluntarily or were forced to die here, did so trying to help each other.

"How old do you think these bones are, Howard?"

"Well, I'm surely no expert, but my guess would be that these were slaves trying to escape into freedom and used the cave for a hiding place. For some reason they couldn't get back outside."

"How awful. What are we going to do?"

"Do? Why would we do anything?"

"Well that wasn't really a question, it was more of an inquiry."

"Inquiry you say." Howard lifted his brow, and looked at Harley suspiciously, "Where I come from that's the same as a question." He set his chin in a stubborn line and said, "So tell me the difference."

"Well, a question is *what* we are going to do with this, but an inquiry is *who* we are going to tell that will investigate?"

"Investigate? You sure do like to stir up trouble, don't ya preacher man. Is that what you do with all those old ladies in your congregation? Like to get them stirred up, huh?"

Not interested in contributing any more to the conversation, Harley turned and began the treacherous walk out of the cave."

"Hold on preacher man, you can't get out of here without the help of my lantern. Besides, we haven't found what we came looking for. You're not going to help me anymore?"

"I would appreciate you getting me out of this dark place and out into the sunlight. We saw nothing to indicate any message on the walls that would help you find your brother. If you want to return, feel free."

Howard lifted his hand in a spirited gesture, pointed toward the front of the cave and walked, gauging his every step. Harley followed, silently concentrating on the footprints in front of him.

Once outside, Harley raised his face to the sky, trying to adjust his eyes to the intensity of the sun's rays. "Sure, feels good out here, don't you think Howard?"

Unexpectedly, quick moving clouds rolled over the sun, causing shadows on the rock formations around the cave entrance. It gave an even more eerie feeling to what they had just experienced.

Harley, walking at a fast pace toward the car, expected Howard to follow him but when he turned around, what he saw brought tears to his eyes. Mr. Tough Guy was still standing at the entrance with his hands shoved in his pockets and his shoulders hunched forward, definitely exhibiting exasperation and hopelessness.

It appeared to Harley that some sort of words should be spoken before he returned to the Inn but saying them out loud didn't seem to be a possibility. Instead, he walked back to Howard, gently laid his hand on the slouching shoulder and began kneading the tense muscles. The watery eyes that turned to look at Harley were now clouded with sadness and a new ruthless determination. Harley slapped him on the back and said, "I'll see you back at the Inn. I'll have a tall glass of tea waiting for you. I think the walk will do you good."

Howard waited until Harley was out of sight, dropped to his knees and wept aloud, rocking back and forth. Terrible regrets assailed him. If only he'd kept in touch with his mother, she might have given him more information about his brother. 'If only' may be just two words but those words formed a huge sentence. The realization of defeat kept him on his knees, holding him immobile. This had been his last attempt and he was ready to quit, yet something kept gnawing at him, telling him not to give up. He soon rose to his feet and began the walk back to the Inn.

Harley and Abby were waiting for him on the front porch, with the promised iced tea.

Abby couldn't contain her excitement as Howard approached the porch steps. "Harley said I have to wait and ask you, Howard, about your discovery. What did you find? Is it something that will help you find your brother?"

"We made a discovery all right, but it has nothing to do with my brother. I'm not sure I'm going to continue the chase. As much as I would like to find him, I'm running low on enthusiasm and emotional strength. Maybe we're just not supposed to meet in this lifetime."

His announcement was unexpected and shocking to Abby. "Howard, you don't mean that!"

"Yes, I do. I've spent the last nine months searching for someone who may not even want to be found. Maybe that's why my mother never told me about him. Why did she wait till the end of her life to tell me something so important?" He turned to face Abby and spoke again, this time with heavy sarcasm resonating in his voice. "Obviously, nurturing wasn't one of my mother's strengths until she found out she was dying and then the guilt became too much to endure. In order for her to die with some sense of peace, she decided to hand over the 'important information', hoping to provoke me into finding my brother. In her mind, I believe she was convinced, by doing so, it relieved her of any parental shame. Informing me at the last minute was probably more intended to be a midnight-hour confession than increasing my number of relatives." Howard was clearly resentful of the situation as he quickly retreated from the porch to his bedroom.

Grief and despair tore at Abby's heart as she moved herself closer to Harley. He wrapped his arm around her shoulders and gave a gentle squeeze. "There's really nothing we can do for him right now. It's something he has to work out on his own." Even though Abby's words were spoken softly and teetering on the edge of wailing, they still carried an underlying steel. "But Harley, you have to help him. Not only is it the right thing to do, but you are a pastor. Isn't that part of your responsibility to people?"

"I have offered to help him as much as I can. I'm not a detective and, to tell you the truth, he's a bit of a hard head. He doesn't take suggestions from strangers very well."

"But we're not strangers. We are all he has right now. How can you not feel some empathy toward him?"

"I do have compassion for him, but my hands are tied as to how I can help find a missing person."

"Technically, he's only missing from Howard's life. Who knows, he could be right here in New Hope. Wouldn't that be something? I wonder if Chief McDonald could help us in any way. I think I'll give him a call."

"I know you want to help Howard, but don't get your hopes up. Besides, this is his crusade and he needs to handle it his way."

Abby took a deep breath and quickly waved aside Harley's coolness. He was the most considerate man she had ever known, but his assessment of Howard was making her uncomfortable. He was acting as if he didn't care.

Ever since Harley had seen Howard sneaking around in the woods, something had intrigued Abby about the stranger. Her first impression was how he carried himself with such self-confidence yet, like a pit bull in a ring, was relentlessly on guard. The remoteness that first surrounded him, like an invisible wall, seemed to allow nothing or no one to penetrate. But hiding behind that façade, she had seen a gentle and kind, quite insecure young man. For the past few weeks she had noticed a small tear in the tent of hopelessness that enclosed him.

CHAPTER 13

Whoever pursues righteousness and kindness will find life, righteousness, and honor.

Proverbs 21:21

Abby stayed true to her assumptions that Chief McDonald could somehow help with Howard's dilemma and called him first thing Monday morning. He seemed genuinely pleased to hear from her and immediately asked how Shirley was doing since her heart attack.

"Well it's difficult to keep her from working so hard, but she's really trying to be a good sport about everything. We're just so glad to still have her around. She gave us quite a scare."

"Please give her my best and tell her to stop in sometime to say hello." He hesitated and then said, "I know you didn't call just to hear my voice, so what can I do for you?"

"I was wondering if I might ask you for a favor or maybe just some advice?"

"I'm listening."

"We have a guest here at the Inn by the name of Howard Douglas. He's in town trying to find information about a brother that he never knew existed, until his mother, on her death bed, revealed the secret. She left him with few words like 'new hope' and 'cave.' We are the last town on the map with the name of 'New Hope' where he hasn't searched. Harley and I have been trying to help but we've run into a dead end. I thought you might suggest what his next steps should be. Howard's very discouraged, but the promise made to his mother is dominating his life."

"How long have you known him? Do you even know if this is a legitimate story?"

"He's only been here a few days but Harley and Shirley believe him too. There's just something about him that opened our hearts and compelled us to support his quest."

"I know how trusting you three at Summer Rain can be, but there are a lot of clever conmen out there these days and you really have to be careful. Before you get too much more involved, let me run a check on him and see if he has any criminal background. Now that we have computers, it's so much easier. A push of a few buttons is all it takes. Do you know where he lived before arriving here?"

"No, that's something he hasn't told us."

"Okay, I'll see what, if anything, I come up with. What was his mother's name?"

"Helen Davis. Howard has no memory of a father so he's not sure where the name Douglas came from and he never had a birth certificate, so he's not even sure where he was born. Shirley asked around and found out about an old cave on the edge of my property so Harley and Howard checked it out."

Abby heard his quick intake of breath. "A cave? You found a cave? What did they expect to find in a cave? Where exactly was this cave?"

"Wow, Tim, sounds like I pushed a hot button. Are you interested in caves or is it just something out of the norm for you?"

"I'm not sure. I haven't heard any reference to caves in this part of the county in a long time but now that you mention it, I remember a story that's been told down through the decades about a group of slaves who disappeared very mysteriously."

"Really?" Abby loved a good mystery and she was definitely interested if it was about local history.

"Local historians say there were a few caves in Carroll County used as hideouts for slaves trying to escape the marauding slave hunters. When the slaves found the natural formations in the side of the mountain, they went in as far as they could to avoid capture. The stories are that they were afraid to come out and eventually died of starvation and cold temperatures. There is documentation that proves these stories are true."

"The cave Harley and Howard found is on the north side of the property. I wonder if it was one of the ill-fated hideaways. Do you think there is any way I could find out?"

"Possibly, but that could be something for the Historical Society to look into. You should talk to Shirley about that. In the meantime, I'll see what I can find out about this Mr. Douglas. I'll get back to you as soon as I know something."

Abby scolded herself for asking so many questions and taking the Chief from his work. Since successfully solving the mysterious death of her husband, Tim McDonald had become a family friend. He and his fiancée, Stacey, were actually planning to be married in the garden of Summer Rain. She did not want to take advantage of their friendship but she totally trusted his judgment and his dedication to finding out the truth, no matter the cost.

Abby heard the lawn mower stop and was happy when she saw Harley coming through the back door. She quickly poured a glass of ice tea and, to his surprise, held it out at arm's length to greet him as he entered the kitchen. He swallowed four big gulps before resting on the bar stool.

"I think the yard gets bigger every week or I guess it could be that I'm just getting older."

She smiled, as though out of pity for him, then her mouth eased into a full-blown grin that she couldn't control. "I'd guess the latter explanation is the real reason for the sweat-soaked shirt." She had to fight the need to be close to him but his sweaty hair and arms were enough to keep her at a distance. "Why don't you get a shower and I'll think about giving you a reward for working so hard."

Harley, still capable of being shocked, stood in pleased surprise. What was she offering him? Did he hear her right? Harley spoke playful words but the meaning was serious. "Just how much of a reward are you planning to give me?"

Abby didn't want to cross over any lines she would regret. She had really only meant a few extra kisses. They had both decided not to be intimate until their wedding night, but it was getting more and more difficult. Now, she had just given Harley the notion that she was ready for the needs she read in his eyes. How could she explain to him that she was just teasing- something she guessed she dare not do.

Abby noticed briefly the "aw shucks" look on his face when she abruptly changed the subject. "Harley, what exactly did you and Howard find in the cave? Howard acted as if it were really something big, yet neither one of you have mentioned it. Why is it such a secret?"

"It's not that it's such a secret, it's just, well, it's a bit gruesome, especially for a lady."

"I'm not a princess, you know. I'm quite capable of handling snags in life. What could be so bad in an old cave."

"We found a pile of bones, human bones to be exact."

"Oh my gosh! Where? How many? Did you find anything else?"

He held up a hand. "Whoa, slow down. I didn't tell you because I thought it would upset you, not excite you."

Abby moved closer to him, her head thrust forward, "I can't believe this. Just this morning, Tim told me about how slaves hid in caves and that it's possible for some of them to be in Carroll County. Now you're saying a cave on our property is a graveyard for people trying to find freedom?"

"It's a possibility."

"How awful, Harley. Tim said I should call the Historical Society and he didn't even know about the bones. What do you think I should do?"

"It's a good idea, might make you feel better. Tell them what you suspect, give them permission to enter the cave and leave the rest up to them."

"You think they'll be able to find out who those people were?"

"I don't know, Abby, but we sure don't have the resources, or the time." He looked directly into her face and winked, "It can be your gift to history."

"Don't make fun of me Harley Davidson. It doesn't become you."

CHAPTER 14

Do not neglect to do good and to share what you have,
for such sacrifices are pleasing to God.

Hebrews 13:16

Lilly had five minutes left on her shift when the jingle bell rang on the diner door. A blush of pleasure rose to her cheeks when she saw it was Warren. With Hoafie trailing behind, of course. He reminded her of a puppy dog following his master. His hair seemed a little rumpled, his eyes sleepy as if he'd just climbed out of bed. Warren was guiding him into the booth near the window, motioning for him to sit.

Ever since the judge had ordered Warren to add an addition to his house and take in Hoafie as part of his community service, life as Warren and Lilly knew it, had changed dramatically. There was very little alone time and even less romantic behavior from Warren. Lilly was practicing patience but some days she felt as if she were competing for his attention. She had a special place in her heart for Hoafie, or as she had nicknamed him, Bear, but Warren was going to have to set some rules or the wedding might be delayed.

Lilly poured Warren his usual cup of coffee, Hoafie's hot chocolate and delivered them to their table. The magnitude of Bear's smile pervaded her and she regretted her thoughts. Deep down she was proud of Warren for the kindness he showed Hoafie and he was no longer the man he used to be. Having a fundamental appreciation of reality kept him grounded. It was comforting, something to hold on to when life got out of hand.

A familiar voice nudged her out of her musings. "Hey, Miss Lilly, thanks for my chocolate."

"You're welcome, Bear. What can I get you to eat this morning?" As she spoke she felt Warren's eyes take in every detail about the way her uniform fit. Pretending not to notice, she continued with Bear's order. When she finally glanced Warren's way, she once again felt the intimate probe of his eyes. He was smiling, not speaking, but she knew what he was thinking, and in her mind, she finished his sentence.

Lilly was so glad today was Wednesday, her short shift of the week. She always looked forward to having extra time to prepare a special meal for her and Warren; it was the one night of the week Hoafie ate alone in his attached apartment. Hoafie needed a tad more independence because he had become quite dependent on his "boss." He also had finally come to accept the fact he had to wait thirty minutes before coming over to Warren's for dinner. That little bit of time gave Warren and Lilly a chance to talk about their day before Hoafie sat down at the table.

Lilly had been home for three hours when she heard the car door slam, and peeking out the window, she saw Hoafie shadowing Warren the entire length of the sidewalk before he veered to the right, toward his own front door.

While he waved his bright blue ball hat, Hoafie smiled and said, 'See ya in thirty, Boss."

"Not tonight, Hoafie, this is Wednesday, remember? I will bring over your food and you can watch TV while you eat. We'll be sure to come over and tell you good night."

Hoafie hung his head and said, "Sorry Boss, I forgot again."

Warren couldn't help but smile as he thought about their predictable rituals, even Hoafie always forgetting about Wednesday nights. He wasn't sure Hoafie's attempt to overlook his 'alone night' wasn't on purpose. Not only did he count on Warren for everyday guidance, but he worshiped the ground Lilly walked on. He would do anything for her. She had taken him under her wing and provided him with motherly love like he had never experienced. He kept asking Warren when they were going to get married so Lilly could live with them all the time. He didn't like the fact that she went back to her apartment every evening.

It made Warren happy that Lilly had accepted Hoafie as part of her life. He was a big responsibility and really, it was Warren's cross to bear, but it was nice to have someone beside him who was willing to help carry the weight.

The rueful acceptance of a terrible knowledge haunted Warren every day. He sometimes still had a hard time believing what he had done. Even though it had carelessly evolved into a tragedy, it was because of the choices he had made in life. The blood from Abby's husband's death would always be on his hands. He took full responsibility, but the guilt that haunted him sometimes overrode any sensible thoughts. With help from a therapist, he was learning to distance himself from the agony of grief, but nothing would ever make him forget.

Lilly thanked God every day for bringing Abby and Harley into their lives. She vividly remembered the day her world had changed from merely surviving to genuine living. Standing beside Warren in church provided her with the safest feeling she had ever known. When the choir began singing "Just as I Am", Warren took her by the hand and together they walked up front. With tears streaming down his cheeks, he knelt in a most humble way. He openly wept, something Lilly never saw a grown man do. Harley joined them and laid a hand on Warren's shoulder, all the while speaking softly about God's love. He spoke of Warren's past sins and how all he had to do was ask and they would be wiped away. Lilly was mesmerized by a message she never heard before. From that day forward, Lilly and Warren walked a different path. The fact that neither had grown up in loving families, made them appreciate the love that church members showed them. They never felt so blessed as when they were among this group of people. Lilly was still a bit skeptical about people who were nice for no reason. Where she came from, that just didn't happen. There was always an ulterior motive.

Warren's bad habit of slamming the door jolted her out of her thoughts. "Lilly, are you home?"

"In the kitchen."

"Before we sit down to dinner, can we talk?"

"Of course. Is everything okay?" Lilly couldn't tell if his behavior was leaning towards annoyance or contentment. His facial expression seemed tense, but it slowly relaxed into a smile and without hesitation, he said, "Oh everything is wonderful."

"Then why the strange face?"

"I guess I'm a bit nervous."

"Warren Wright, quit beating around the bush and tell me what's wrong with you!"

"Nothing. I just want to ask you something."

"Then ask it!"

His voice was choked with sincerity when he finally spoke. "I love you, Lillian Nicole Fisher. I want to marry you as soon as possible. How about tomorrow?"

"Oh no, you're not getting away that cheap. You promised me the wedding of my dreams and I'm holding you to it."

"Then start planning because I can't wait much longer. Let's go see Abby and Harley so we can set a date."

A great rejoicing filled Lilly's chest as she laced her fingers around Warren's neck and began to cry. He didn't have to ask her twice.

CHAPTER 15

Forget the former things; do not dwell on the past.

Isaiah 43:18

S ince Shirley's heart attack, answering the phone had become her chief assignment at Summer Rain. It was a very important role but didn't require a lot of physical activity. She had a way of putting people at ease the minute she said 'hello'. Abby did not miss this task, since her former job in the loan department had consisted of telephone talk most days. She enjoyed talking to people but talking about money had become mundane. She now looked forward to Shirley beckoning her to the phone, knowing it was a personal call. Today, such a call from Warren Wright was just what she needed. It had been a few months since she and Harley had heard from Warren and Lilly. She assumed they had been busy fulfilling the court order to build an addition to their house for Hoafie. The Judge also declared Warren to be Hoafie's custodian for as long as he lived. She knew Warren was still having nightmares from the role he played in her husband's death. Technically, Jeff was murdered and Warren was a part of it, even though he had been totally unaware of his involvement. Hoafie, an incredible, loyal employee to Warren, carried out his intoxicated boss's wishes, thinking he was doing a great deed. Not that cutting brake lines was the norm for him but doing anything to a car made Hoafie happy. The judge, considering Hoafie's mental capacity and all of the circumstances surrounding the situation, awarded guardianship of Hoafie to Warren, as part of his community service requirement. It meant no jail time for Warren and Hoafie, and allowed Hoafie to have his own space. Lilly had come to love the gentle giant, waiting on him hand and foot, and in turn, she always received the biggest smile she ever saw on a human face.

Warren and Lilly were planning to get married at Summer Rain and Abby hoped the phone call was concerning the date and time.

"Hi Abby. I know this is short notice but Lilly and I were wondering if we could come out today to talk about the wedding?"

Abby let out a squeal and a giggle. "You don't know how long I've been waiting for this phone call. I can't wait to see what you two want to do, as far as decorations and so forth."

"That is definitely yours and Lilly's department. I know she is bursting at the seams to get started on the planning. We've been trying to get Hoafie settled in before we jump into another undertaking. Although; this one I'm looking forward to."

"Please come out to the Inn today. I'll have the coffee and tea ready. We need some catch and release time."

"And what exactly would that be?"

"We need to catch up on the news from the past few months and release some of the latest announcements, like your wedding!"

Warren roared with laughter that rumbled deep in his chest. "See you in a little while, Abby."

Abby quickly retrieved all the wedding planner books she had purchased. Maps from the cave search had to be folded and put away before she could spread out magazines and dress design books on the table in the sunroom. Obviously, this was going to be her go-to planning room.

The sun came through the large windows, like a giant magnet pulling you in, warming not only your body, but your heart as well. The soothing rays seemed to alleviate the stress of everyday problems. It was a peaceful setting for making decisions.

When the doorbell rang, Abby practically ran to open it. She and Lilly embraced immediately but Warren was a bit hesitant. He still felt a lot of regret about what happened to Abby's husband, Jeff. He knew she had forgiven him but a fragment of shame still resided in a corner of his heart. He had killed many men during the Vietnam war, but somehow this was different. There, he had been provided with a weapon and ordered to destroy. Here, he had freely chosen his weapon of destruction - alcohol. Any time he now had an urge to take a drink, an image of Abby and the grief he caused, came flashing before his eyes. It was actually worse than remembering battles with the enemy.

Each time Abby was near Warren, a memory of her husband ruffled through her mind like wind on water. She actually felt herself flinch, resenting his familiarity. She was confident she truly forgave him, but she wasn't sure she would ever be able to forget. The only way to bypass the ache was to immerse her thoughts into her current surroundings. Right now, Warren was standing in front of her looking very uncomfortable. It was her job, if only because she was owner of the Inn, to make him feel at ease. Lilly stood there as if fastened to the wall, waiting for Abby to invite them in. When she didn't, Lilly seized the moment and nudged Warren's elbow to make way for her to move towards Abby and gracefully give her a hug. Grateful for the distraction, Abby smiled and responded with an embrace.

The slump in Warren's shoulders quickly began to relax and before he realized it, he was clutching her hand with both of his. "Thank you, Abby this means a lot to Lilly and I. Sorry we didn't give you more notice but we're really getting anxious."

"No worries Warren. I have everything laid out in the sunroom, waiting for your approval."

CHAPTER 16

For I know the plans I have for you, declares the Lord,
plans for welfare and not for evil, to give you
a future and a hope.

Jeremiah 29:11

Lilly couldn't stop smiling when she saw the display Abby had spread out on the table. How was she ever going to make a decision? There were at least fifty pictures of wedding dresses and stacks of magazines with photos of outdoor weddings. Abby seemed to be in her element with all of this, and Lilly was so grateful for her help, but she just wanted simple and elegant. It would be a small wedding since she had no living relatives that she knew of, and Warren's relatives were also very few. It would mostly be friends to help them celebrate their special day.

Abby poured each of them a glass of tea and placed a plate of freshly-made cookies in front of them.

"So, tell me Lilly, do you know what you want or are you just here to look?"

"The only thing I know is that I want it simple but still elegant."

"Great. Let's go outside and I'll show you the gazebo and a few other special areas that we think you will like."

In the end, Lilly and Warren decided on the gazebo, simply because it was beautiful. Ivy had twined its way to the top of the lattice work, giving the structure a cottage feel. It was perfect. Exactly what Lilly wanted. The rest of the evening was spent finishing the final details. Everything from the flowers to the food. Harley and Warren enjoyed the front porch while Lilly chose her wedding dress from the many designs of the season. She settled on a strapless pearl white dress with an eye-catching side-swept ruffle and a bold, crystal embellishment at the hip, which accentuated her thin waist. She began to cry when she realized this was really happening and not just one of her fantasies. As a young girl, she had stolen magazines from wherever she could, just to cut out the pictures of wedding dresses, especially the Oscar de la Renta designs. She had pasted them into a notebook but one of her mother's boyfriends found it and made her cut it into small pieces. In the breathy voice of an alcoholic, he made fun of her the entire time she was cutting. Each piece she dropped into the trash can was just another piece of her dreams crushed by a man. But that was in the past and she was now planning a future with Warren- a wonderful man whom she knew would never humiliate her or restrain her from dreaming. As a child, fantasizing about a designer wedding gown was probably hollow and jagged with conflict, but to Lilly, it represented hope and gave her the desire to aspire to a better life. A designer gown was no guarantee that life would be perfect, but at the time, she had needed something to hold on to and pictures of the dresses had provided her with just that.

Abby went to call the local bridal shop about the availability of the dress, and on her return, found Lilly softly crying, yet smiling comfortably to herself. "What's wrong Lilly? Are you crying or smiling?"

"A little of both. I'm so overwhelmed with happiness that it's making me cry."

Abby laughed at the sight of her friend. How wonderful to be so blissfully happy and so fully alive. "I hope this will make you even happier. You have an appointment tomorrow morning with Mrs. Devoe at the bridal shop."

"Abby you are coming with me, aren't you?"

"Try stopping me!"

There seemed to be a psychic link between these two women and they startled giggling. As if on cue, Harley and Warren returned to the room just in time to see the two women do a sort of victory dance, which caused the two men to do a long, slow slide with their eyes. What was it about women and weddings? Sometimes Warren wished he had not promised Lilly the wedding of her dreams. He would be happy just standing in front of the Justice of the Peace at the courthouse. But then other times, like now, as he watched the joy on Lilly's face, he felt a smile of pure pleasure spread across his face. Of all the women he had shared time with, Lilly was the only solid reality in his shifting world. Not exactly raised in the embrace of high society, her compulsive lust for life was contagious. Her smile alone, made his spirits soar with shameless delight, no matter the circumstances. He was learning how not to be depressed, a wonderful emotion he had never experienced until getting to know Lilly. Still watching her, he found all his emotions agreeable. Yes, she was beautiful, yes, she was smart and yes, how did he get so lucky? From the first day he met Lilly he had recognized a built-in sense of social grace, one he found quite alluring. Had he known that she had found him attractive, he would have responded sooner to her flirting, which he mistook for waitress friendly bantering.

At the sound of Lilly's voice, Warren lifted his head. She had moved next to him and was brushing her fingers over his collar and the ends of his hair. "I've been talking to you and I don't think you've heard a word I said. Are you all right?"

Gratitude choked him, almost to the point of not being able to talk. He grinned and let out a long, low whistle. "I just enjoy watching your enthusiasm over something only a woman gets excited about."

"Warren! It's our wedding. How can you not be happy?"

Grinning in a distinctly male-satisfaction sort of way, he said softly, "Didn't say I wasn't happy, just don't understand all the frenzy about some clothes and decorations."

The magnetism of his smile drew her closer to his face and she kissed the tip of his nose. "Since this stuff is so boring, why don't you go outside with Harley and find something to do."

Warren watched as she walked toward the sunroom, enjoying the gentle sway of her hips.

Chapter 17

"Thanks for the breakfast, Abby. I have some research in town today so I'm not sure when I'll be back."

"It's okay, Howard. You're a free man around here. You don't have to tell me your schedule." Abby smiled as she added, "Your consideration though, is appreciated."

Howard walked out of the kitchen and slowly down the hall toward the front door, hoping Abby would remember he didn't have a car. Sure enough, she came hurrying behind him, asking him to wait. "How are you getting to town?"

"I was planning on walking, hoping someone would stop and give me a ride."

Abby held up the collection of keys and shook them gently. "Take my car. I won't need it today and it appears that you do."

Howard smiled as he accepted her gift.

Walking into the library brought back memories of his foster days. The smell of books and the warmth of the sun coming in through the big windows reminded him of the few times he had gone with his temporary family to pick up or return books. Walking between the long rows of books, from floor to ceiling, had created a safe haven for him, allowing him to get lost in the titles and the dreams of faraway places. Maybe he could indulge in that feeling today for a while before he began his research. He had no idea how to operate a computer, but the library advertised that they would provide an instructor, if requested.

He moseyed back and forth past the book laden shelves hoping for a title to jump out at him, begging him to remove it from the shelf, something he hadn't done in a long, long time. Today for some reason, his reading skills seemed to be joining forces with his need for adventure. Huckleberry Finn, a book he had been required to read in school, but never had, came into view and he pulled the book from the shelf. A small opening to the other side was created and looking back at him was the most stunning, yet sad, set of eyes he had ever seen. He smiled, and the penetrating eyes, mirroring the color of the sky, instantly disappeared. Curious, Howard moved toward the end of the row, turned the corner expecting to see the girl, but there was no one in sight. He looked all around but it was as if she disappeared into the air. He made his way to the front desk and asked the clerk if she had seen anyone leave the library.

"Obviously you aren't from around here." The middle-aged woman's eyebrows rose a trifle as she examined Howard's appearance.

"No, I've only been here a few weeks. Is there something I should know?"

The lady's eyebrows rose again, this time in amazement. "It's not something you have to know, it's just that everyone who lives here knows who she is."

"Well, I don't know, so are you going to tell me?"

With an annoyed expression she declared, "I'm not the town gossip you know. I really feel sorry for that young lady. She's extremely intelligent but she's never had a chance in life."

"So, what's her story?"

"Like I said, I'm not the town gossip but I can tell you this. She is a recluse and only comes to town on Monday mornings. I've tried to befriend her but she just won't talk to anyone. Even me, who she sees every week. Rumors have been around town about her family but I guess no one really knows the truth and I guess no one ever took the time to find out. She lives alone on the north side of town, next to the mountain, and again, rumor has it that she knows how to use a shotgun. Her name is Freedom." Without interruption, she asked Howard if he would be checking out any books today.

"No, but I'll be back."

As he walked out the door and down the wide marble steps, he wondered about this girl named Freedom. How ironic to have a name that meant independence and yet be confined to a life of solitude. He could easily relate to her way of life. Even though he always seemed surrounded by people, he identified with loners.

On his way back to Summer Rain his mind began challenging his heart. Why was he even thinking about a girl he had only seen for a split second? He had no idea how the rest of her looked. She might be uglier than sin and she might weigh more than him. He had been picky over the last ten years about his women. He got to pick and choose and he cared only about their physical appearance. He wasn't interested in how the brain or heart operated, only that the body performed to his satisfaction. He didn't feel worthy of being loved, and truthfully, he wasn't even sure what the word meant. His own mother hadn't been able to love him so she gave the responsibility to someone else. King was the closest thing to a father he ever knew, but when he truly thought about their relationship, he realized that he was nothing more to King than a card counter in a casino. Deep down he knew he had traded his soul for recklessness and, for what it was worth, the desire to be loved.

In the beginning, King convinced him that he thought of him as a son and Howard, wanting that fatherly love, was naive enough to believe him. He realized too late that King was only using him. He had tried many times to remember his real father, Hank, to compare the two, but he didn't have enough memory to be able to evaluate and parallel something so important. Looking back, Howard was sure of one thing: King had no understanding of parental love. As time went on, Howard began to feel cheaper than tattoos. He had to learn to distance himself from the humiliation and pain King dumped on him day after day. With limited skills, he felt he had no choice but to continue working for King. Howard persevered inside the noisy walls of casinos twelve hours a day, sometimes with no breaks. Even though there were no physical chains attached to him, the casinos were King's grasslands and everyone knew he was the bull. Jumping the fence and escaping was not an option. And because of that, Howard came to terms with his situation. And besides, what else in life did he have to do.

It was quite a shock when he got word that his mother was still alive, dying in a hospital, asking for him. King, whose mother died years before, felt a sentimental twinge when he heard the news. It triggered his one and only bit of decency. When he gave Howard permission to visit his mother in the hospital, it was like unlocking the gate. Not until his mother's last words did Howard comprehend his chance for escape from the grasslands.

Because he was so submerged in memories, he actually lost track of how close he was to home. He had put the window down, liking the feel of the fresh air blowing his hair. Obviously, the breeze had shifted to the south because he smelled smoke and wet leaves. He realized he was close to the Inn, which meant that Harley must be burning leaves today. He pulled off to the side of the road, got out of his car and weaved his way through the trees until he found Harley vigorously raking leaves into the fire. Harley was dressed in faded wrangler jeans with battered, low heeled boots he used to kick small rocks out of the way. He nearly fell backwards into the fire when Howard emerged from behind a tree.

"Next time you decide to sneak up on someone you might want to give a little bit of notice. We all might live longer. What are you doing out here?'

"First of all, I wasn't sneaking, and secondly, I thought maybe you could use a little help."

"Really? There is another rake in the shed and while you're there could you bring the cart? I need to load up these ashes and put them on the compost pile."

"Looks like you're really into this outdoor stuff. I've never had the opportunity to see if I like it or not."

"Well now's your chance. Maybe with your help, I'll finish this today."

Howard found his way back to the car and pulled in to the rear parking lot, near the shed. He took the rake from the wall, threw it inside the cart and hurried back to Harley.

While the last of the leaves were burning, Howard could not stop himself from wondering. "Harley, have you ever heard of a girl by the name of Freedom who lives next to the mountain on the north side?"

"Can't say that I have, why?"

"I caught a glimpse of her today at the library and when I asked the clerk about her I got a hazy description. I'd just like to know her story."

"If that's what you want to know, I suggest you go talk to Shirley. She's the historian around here."

CHAPTER 18

For you were called to freedom, brothers. Only do not use your freedom as an opportunity for the flesh, but through love serve one another.

Galatians 5:13

Howard found Shirley in the kitchen brewing a new pot of coffee. "Good afternoon Howard. Are you in need of a cup of coffee?"

"That sounds great and while I'm enjoying your brew I was wondering if you could answer a few questions for me?"

"Ask away."

"Do you know anything about the girl named "Freedom" who lives near the mountain?"

Shirley's aging body turned slowly toward Howard, a gleam of interest in her eyes. "Freedom? You're asking about Freedom Hunter?"

"Hunter? Her last name is Hunter? Why would a parent name their child Freedom when their last name is Hunter?"

Shirley raised the coffee cup to her lips and took a long sip. She took her time answering because it was a long time since she had thought about the Hunter family.

Howard sensed Shirley's reply was going to be quite the tale, so he sat back and waited.

"First of all, Howard, how do you know about Freedom and why are you asking?"

"I saw her at the library and the clerk didn't seem to know anything about her except for the rumors she heard. I pulled a book from the shelf and a sad pair of eyes looked at me from the other side. I saw something so familiar in those eyes. There was an agitated look, like someone in pain."

"She *is* in pain Howard, but it's emotional pain. Let me tell you what I know. Her parents, John and Effie Hunter were flower children left over from the days of Woodstock. They never quite got over being groupies and they were high most of the time on marijuana. John grew up here in New Hope, on the farm where Freedom now lives. He was an only child and so when his parents died, he, of course, inherited the farm. He also received quite a sum of money from the estate so he never felt the need to work. Most of the money was spent on pot, in fact they eventually grew their own until the field was discovered by a hunter. When Effie gave birth, the word freedom endorsed their 'hippie' behavior, so having a kid named Freedom Hunter kept them in that classic paradigm of 'we can do it our way'."

Shirley took a deep breath and continued. "Freedom was around nine or ten years old when her mother died from an overdose. By that time, she had learned to take care of herself. She even managed to get to school on her own and do household chores. John blamed himself for Effie's death and before long he lost control of his anger and hurt. He began drinking heavily, basically leaving Freedom to fend for herself. One morning before school she found her dad lying in a pool of blood out by the barn. Story was that he had been drunk, fell and hit his head on a rock. The coroner ruled it an accident. By that time Freedom was old enough to legally live alone and that's what she's been doing ever since. She raises beef cattle, sells a few every fall and she sells vegetables from her garden, to the local stores. Considering her upbringing she's quite the entrepreneur."

Shirley took another sip of coffee and resumed her story. "Freedom has never had a friend. In school, she was constantly made fun of. She had very few dresses and those she did have were hand-me-downs from her mother that she altered herself. She was always quite artistic and could do incredible things with a needle. I've heard she has turned her parents' scant wardrobe into some beautiful quilts."

Shirley watched Howard's face as she talked, and was pleased to see, even though he had a look of disbelief, she noted compassion in his eyes. He hadn't interrupted yet so she maintained her enthusiasm with, "When John began drinking he also became abusive. The only freedom in that household was his daughter's name. She was for sure a prisoner. When she got a little older, he used guilt to keep her there. Basically, she was his slave. There was nothing the sheriff could do unless Freedom filed a complaint, and she would never do that. The day her daddy died was the first day her name ever really held any truth for her. But some say it's too late. She knows no other way of life. She has probably read every book in the library. Reading served as an escape and she is still avoiding real life. She only leaves the farm to buy a few groceries and to visit the library. And it's sad to say, but since there is no more scandal, people have just forgotten about her. I'm ashamed to say that includes me, too."

Howard made no effort to speak, but simply rose from his chair and walked out the door.

Shirley watched out the window as he marched toward Harley, said a few words and returned to Abby's car. Within seconds he was speeding down the highway.

When Betty looked up from filing library cards she was startled to see Howard waiting at the counter. "Can I help you?"

"I hope so. I talked to you earlier about the girl named Freedom. Could you please tell me how to get to her farm?"

She leaned forward and lowered her voice. "I know where she lives but I'm not allowed to give out that kind of information."

Howard squinted, peering around the room. "Doesn't seem to be anyone around, and besides, would anyone really care?"

Betty shot him a sarcastic glance but pulled a card from the file and laid it on the counter. Howard pretended not to see it but memorized the address. Pausing, he gazed at her, "One more thing, beautiful, how do I get there?"

Betty's smile was disarmingly generous as she jotted down the directions. Howard blew her a kiss and disappeared through the front door.

It didn't take him long to find Freedom's farm even though the driveway was obscured from the road. It was the most run-down property he had ever seen. The barn door was barely attached, windows were broken out and parts of the roof were already caved in. A few chickens and guineas were pecking the ground. He didn't know much about either one but he assumed they were looking for something to eat. Some cows lingered under a tree as if hiding from the sun while a small donkey stood sleeping.

Everywhere he looked, he saw work waiting to happen. The house, a large two-story gray stone with a peaked slate roof showed numerous indications that the house had weathered many storms. The few pieces of slate that hadn't blown off were so faded they almost matched the color of the stone. The back side of the roof sagged, like bread when taken out of the oven too soon. The limestone, on all sides, was streaked with the drippage of the leaky gutters that ran along the edge of the roof. The wide shutters thrown back from the windows were rotting from the hinges and barely hanging on. Chips of white paint lay scattered on the sills like dandruff. Inside, curtains the color of the sun, hung abundantly, as if their weight would prevent the outside elements from entering. Green moss and ivy clung wildly to the outer walls, adding character to the once attractive home. The grass, no longer a vibrant green, was in dire need of attention.

Howard didn't know how long he'd stood there assessing the damage, when he felt something pushing against his back.

"Don't know who you are, mister, but you better git."

Howard spoke slowly, feeling his way. "My name is Howard Douglas. I'm staying out at the Inn on Route 6. I saw you today at the library. I know your name is Freedom and it looks like you could use a little help around here." He felt the thrust of the hard metal dig deeper into his back. He slowly raised his hands in the air, waiting for a verbal response, but got none. He closed his eyes and winced as the coldness touched his neck, causing goosebumps. Afraid to speak, he waited. Before he knew what was happening, he felt the same icy heaviness on his forehead. He bravely opened his eyes to find himself staring into the barrel of a sawed-off shotgun. The eyes behind the metal seemed to express more challenge than curiosity.

She spoke in a neutral way, without inflection, "Who sent you out here?"

"I told you, I saw you today at the library. We saw each other through the opening in the books, remember? I'm looking for work and I was told you might be able to help me."

She double-checked her memory and yes, he was the set of eyes from the library. She gave him a quick glance. "Work? You don't look like you've worked a day in your life."

Ignoring her he quietly said, "I do not wear my working clothes when I go to town, especially the library. It has always been a safe place for me and out of respect, I would not step foot inside wearing dirty or ugly clothes."

With a little smart-ass grin, she stepped back, still pointing the gun, "Did you by any chance, look in a mirror before you left your house today? Because if you did, you obviously need glasses. That has to be the most hideous sweater I've ever seen on a man before."

Howard's lips trembled with the need to smile. Finally, he gave in, and it was a deep, honest laugh, good-natured and sincere.

Freedom blew out a breath and moved another step away from him. He was laughing at her but not the kind of laugh that belittles a person. It sounded sincere, good humored. So different than she had ever heard before and she found it impossible not to return his charismatic smile.

"Can I put my hands down now?" he asked, still smiling.

She promptly disengaged her finger from the trigger and leaned the gun against the nearest tree.

Dropping his hands, Howard stepped back, not sure what would happen next. To his surprise, she turned and walked towards the house. Not knowing what else to do, he followed her. She held the screen door open as he entered the kitchen, which smelled like fresh roses. Everywhere he looked he saw mason jars filled with bouquets of all colors. It was like walking into an old-time florist shop. He helped himself to a chair and sat down, pretending he was invited.

Freedom took note of his quiet composure and wondered exactly what it was he was thinking and why he had sought her out. Was he really here because he needed a job or did he plan to steal the antiques that people claimed she owned? He seemed too young to be interested in vintage but God only knew what he had heard in town. There were all sorts of rumors. With her own ears she heard people talking about her while she lingered behind a row of books. The lady at the library tried to befriend her, telling her to never mind the things she overheard. The only people she had ever trusted, had let her down and now she didn't want to trust anyone. So why had she let this complete stranger into her house? She never allowed any visitors to come inside.

Ever since she had encountered Howard on the other side of the books, she thought about him and now here he was, sitting on her kitchen chair, staring at her. The only man who ever captivated her before was her father, even when he was falling down drunk and abusive. She had idolized him and did her best to be his 'little princess' but after her mother's death he no longer treated her as royalty. He was mean and couldn't be bothered with someone who reminded him of his wife. He blamed himself and found company in his misery. He had no more use for a princess. When he died, Freedom withdrew from society and allowed the townspeople to determine her fate. They judged her as a human being who was broken, abused, and who, ultimately, was crazy. She tolerated their judgment and became a recluse.

Now she stood in front of a man who was obviously waiting for her to speak and she had no idea what to say or even how to act. He drummed his nails on the table, making a noise like pigeons' feet on the roof. She could hear the hanging clothes outside making soft, snapping sounds in the breeze. And yet, there was the roar of absolute silence. But she went on, blithely ignoring the sounds.

"Would you like something to drink?"

Howard looked up, flashing a smile of thanks. "Thought you'd never ask."

CHAPTER 19

*Let each of you look not only to his own interests,
but also, to the interests of others.*

Philippians 2:4

Shirley was sitting at the piano in the sunroom when she saw Howard park Abby's car in the rear parking lot. She watched as he pushed away from the car, went into the woods and soon came toward the house. Sensing some anxiety, she met him in the hallway.

Trying to sound compassionate, Shirley inquired gently, "You went to see Freedom, didn't you?"

"Why would you say that?"

"Because I'm a woman with great intuition. What did you think of her?"

"I thought she was beautiful."

The tenderness in his expression amazed her. "Well now, that's an answer I wasn't expecting, but I can't say I'm surprised."

"I thought you didn't really know her?"

"I don't, but I knew her mother, and when she wasn't high, she was sweeter than honey. Her hair was honey colored, too."

"Why didn't anyone try to help Freedom after her mother died?"

"Oh, lots of people tried, but everyone who tried to come on the property was met with a shotgun."

"Wow! I guess like father, like daughter."

Shirley couldn't control her burst of laughter. "And you still think she's beautiful? Must have been quite the visit."

"It was a little scary at first, but for some reason she warmed up to me and we ended up having some mint tea together. I'm going back out there tomorrow and I'm going to do some work around the place. I'm not sure exactly what to do first, but I guess I'll figure it out when I get there."

Abby entered the room just then and asked who they were talking about. Shirley related the saga as best she could until Abby interrupted with a plea, "Let me go with you tomorrow, Howard. Sounds like she could use another woman's company."

"I don't think that's a good idea, Abby. She's really skittish. I think we should let her get used to just me and then maybe I can take you out later to meet her."

Pushing her bottom lip forward in thought, Abby insisted Howard take a batch of freshly-baked cookies to his new friend. "When you think she's ready to meet me, please let me know."

Howard fell into a vague half sleep that night, drifting in a bed of roses only to fall from a ladder, surrounded by cattle. Men with pointed guns and a brown-haired cupid were shooting arrows at his heart. Stacks of cards swirled around his head as liquor flowed freely from the mountainside. He woke several times, relentlessly haunted by the same images. By morning, he was exhausted and sensed the need for more sleep but the thought of seeing Freedom overrode the temptation.

Shirley and Abby anticipated Howard's early rise and had eggs and bacon waiting for him as he tried to sneak into the kitchen.

"What are you two doing up so early?"

"We might ask you the same question!"

"I smelled the bacon and had to come down. What's the occasion?"

Abby and Shirley looked at each other and grinned in amusement.

"What? Why are you two smiling? What's so funny?"

Shirley's voice broke as she tried to say, "Oh, nothing is funny, it's just cute."

"Cute? Nothing about me is cute! What's wrong with you two this morning?"

Abby couldn't help herself, "You're going out to help Freedom, today aren't you?"

Seeing their mouths twitch with amusement, he smiled, causing featherlike laugh lines to crinkle around his eyes as he spoke, "Oh so that's what this is about. Women are always looking for a way to create gossip, aren't they? I didn't think you two would stoop to that level."

Abby's voice, suddenly dripping with southern richness, exclaimed, "Gossip? Whatever do you mean? We're just trying to decide which garden we can use for your wedding."

Howard nearly choked on his piece of toast. "Wedding? You two don't know me very well. I'm not the marrying kind. I just usually love'em and leave'em. Easier that way. And besides, why would I want to get involved with a girl that everyone says is crazy?" He took a drink of coffee and continued, "No thanks. I just saw her place as an opportunity to practice my hand at restoration, a new subject for me. Besides, I'm sure you're tired of seeing me around here all day. I need to do something constructive and a little jingle in my pocket wouldn't hurt, either." He grabbed his coffee cup and managed to get out the door before either woman could respond.

Harley opened the back door and was greeted with side-splitting laughter from Abby and Shirley. It seemed contagious and before long he, too, was laughing a real hard, solid laugh. But why? He had, some time ago, accepted the fact that a woman's natural state was mysterious, while men have a natural respect for consistent behavior. This was like walking into the female hyena cage at the zoo. And he, for some reason, was joining in. The sound of his own voice scared him as he tried to shout louder than the dueling hyenas. Finally, there was only the sound of the drip from the coffee pot and the hum of the refrigerator. "What are you two so hysterical about?"

"Who's hysterical? We're just having a little fun. Would you like to get in on the bet, Pastor Harley?"

"Running against the current of the church aren't you, ladies? And exactly what are you betting on?

"Howard's smitten with Freedom Hunter. He's on his way out there right now. Says he's gonna do some work." Abby stared at Shirley and once again burst out laughing.

By this time Harley was totally confused. Who was Freedom Hunter and why was Howard looking for work? Did that mean he was planning to stay in New Hope?

Harley looked at Abby and said, "Are you going to fill me in?"

"Sorry dear, but I have to run. Maybe Shirley will have time." She blew Harley a kiss as she went through the door and said, "See you two later. I'll be home late this afternoon."

Shirley told Harley as much of the story about Freedom that she knew to be fact and then added the many rumors that had drifted around during the years. In spite of his tenacity, Harley's mind inevitably returned to the time when rumors had earmarked him as a thief. He mused on some private memories, his face turning sober, for he knew how it felt to be branded as something you're not. He was thankful for the steadfastness of his faith, knowing God would deliver him from the battle.

He didn't know about this girl, but now that he did, he would do what he could to help her, both spiritually and emotionally.

CHAPTER 20

When the righteous triumph, there is great glory,
But when the wicked rise, men hide themselves.

Proverbs 28:12

"This is Spencer Kingsley. I've been waiting to hear some news on that subject I called you about last week. I don't like to wait. Is there a problem?"

"A slight one sir. We still haven't located Mr. Douglas. I have my whole team on it but they've come up with nothing. It's as if he fell off the earth."

"I can tell you who's going to fall off the earth if you don't find him soon. I'm a man of little to no patience, Mr. Morgan, and if you don't find him soon, I hope you like your new planet. You've got one week to find him. Good day." There was a stalking, purposeful intent in King's walk as he moved out of his office door.

Lou Morgan felt white starbursts of pain moving through his brain just thinking about the damage King would do to his body. He saw, first hand, the mutilation of men who crossed King. Just because he was a private detective didn't mean he could solve every case and he had tried to tell that to King but to no avail. Now he was faced with a deadline and no feasible leads. If he went to the police he would be a dead man within hours. King had eyes everywhere. Lou never had a problem working with King until now. Previous jobs had dealt only with domestic problems caused by his employees' wives. A scorned woman was rather easy to find. He discovered that in order to find out local news, he need only to get a haircut. Sitting in a salon was a most entertaining way to obtain information for which he didn't ask. But this, this was different. This young man could be anywhere in the United States. Running out on King would be a sure death sentence. The further away he had run, the better his chances of vanishing. But that also meant Lou couldn't find him either.

A dream, or maybe he should've called it a vision, came to him in the middle of the night. A girl named Lucy Fletcher seemed to be calling his name. He hadn't thought of her in years. She was a contact of his when he lived on the east coast. But, why was he thinking of her now? He had lost track of her when he moved out west and she never tried to contact him since his relocation.

Lou sat down with a cup of coffee and concentrated on why this woman's name came to mind now. He assumed she still lived in Virginia but he remembered she had a lot of contacts in Chicago and that's where Howard's mother had died. Maybe he should call her. But what could she possibly know? He didn't even know if she was still alive or even if she lived in the same place. He found her number in an old address book and dialed. He left a message, asking her to call him.

A day of gray unrest, apprehension and a faint, though distant nervous anxiety hounded Lou till he felt unsettling fluttering's pricking his chest. He needed to hear from Lucy. It was his only chance. If she didn't call him, he might as well start planning his funeral. He was out of options.

When the phone finally rang, Lou hesitated, fearing it might be King, but the voice on the other end was definitely a woman. "Is this Lou Morgan?"

"Yes, Lucy, it's me. Thank you for returning my call. I need your help. Do you still have any contacts in the Chicago area?"

"Yes, I still know some people. What are you trying to find out?"

"I'm looking for a man named Howard Douglas. His mother died at Chicago General less than a year ago. He never returned to his job and his boss has hired me to find him. I'm trying to find a way to warn the young man that Kingsley Spencer is trying to find him, because if he does, he will kill him."

"Kingsley Spencer! How did you get caught up working for that creep?"

"Oh, so you've heard of him. Someday, when we have a lot of time, I'll tell you, but time is of the essence right now, so do you think you can help me?"

"Give me a couple of days and I'll get back to you. I feel confident I can get you enough information to find this kid." She paused, then ended their conversation with, "Good to hear from you, Lou. I'll be in touch."

By the end of the conversation, Lou was convinced divine intervention had produced Lucy's name. He now felt a ringing impulse of hope.

Two days later, Lucy faxed the name of New Hope, North Carolina to Lou, along with the name of Summer Rain. She ended it with, "Keep in touch", Lucy.

Lou could usually handle any situation and remain unfazed but, standing there reading Lucy's message, his gut clenched with one of his intuitions that never forecast anything good. He hated working for King but he was more afraid to go against him. The king's requests, up until now, had been simple commands to Lou, but this one could mean life or death. Maybe even his own.

By contract, he was obligated to disclose Howard's location, but with regard to his conscience, he realized he also had a responsibility to the young man who had escaped King's claws. He had no doubt King would slither into the town and Howard would be looking into the eyes of Satan without warning. He had to find him before he gave King this information.

He called Lucy again, explained the situation and once again she volunteered her assistance. "I'll call you when the mission is completed." Had he been able to see her he would have seen the two perfect dimples formed in her cheeks by her smile.

Lucy decided to own this assignment. It was awhile since she had been down south and this sounded like a perfect opportunity for a vacation. She had names and locations, so how hard could it be to give someone a warning? Besides, Lou seemed a bit edgy about this one and she hoped she could put his mind at ease.

As Lucy drove through the town of New Hope, she thought about how peaceful the streets seemed, with their hanging pots overflowing with greenery and blooming flowers. Lots of benches sat beneath trees, waiting for someone to occupy them. The sidewalks were somewhat deserted, but those who were window shopping were actually taking time to speak to other shoppers. An unladylike growl came from the pits of her stomach just as she saw the sign for Big George's Diner. She pulled into the parking spot and hurried inside. A pleasant waitress named Lilly appeared at her table with the menu and silverware. She ordered French toast and a cup of tea. Feeling that Lilly would be a good source of information she asked, "Do you happen to know how I can get to Summer Rain Bed & Breakfast?"

To Lilly, this was an invitation to talk about her wedding. "Summer Rain? I sure can tell you how to get there. It's where I'm getting married next week. You're gonna love it. It's a beautiful house and the gardens are spectacular. Are you going to stay a few days?"

Lucy smiled, knowing that she obviously asked the right person. "I'm just passing through so I'm not sure how long I'll be staying. I heard about this Summer Rain and I thought I would check it out."

"Oh, you won't be disappointed. The owners, Abby and Miss Shirley, well, you are going to love them. They are the best." She broke off with an apology, "I'm sorry. I shouldn't be rambling on, it's just that I'm a bit excited."

"As you should be. I'm looking forward to meeting Abby and Shirley. Thanks so much for the information."

Lucy finished her breakfast and followed Lilly's directions to the Inn. The waitress was right. These two women were delightful and she felt an instant connection. She had no doubt about their sincerity, so she enlightened them both with details about her search.

Shirley's face collapsed into a complex set of wrinkles while Abby's fell in disappointment. She got used to Howard's presence and now to think that he might be forced back to an immoral life or worse yet, be killed. Didn't this kind of thing only happen in the city?

Shirley was quick to speak, "We are here to help you any way we can. What do you want us to do?"

"I need to see Howard here, where he's comfortable. I don't want to spook him and make him run."

Shirley spoke up again, "He's out at the old Hunter farm doing some work and he usually comes back around six. We can get you all settled in nicely before he comes home and then after dinner you can strike up a private conversation with him. Pastor Harley will also be here this evening so if you'd like, he can run interference for you after you talk to Howard."

"Pastor Harley?"

"Yes, he and Abby are friends. He dines with us quite often". She flaunted a wink and added, "If you know what I mean!"

Lucy smiled and quietly said, "I think I do. I'll be grateful for any help you can give me with this, but I would appreciate that nothing be said to Howard. His life could be in danger and anyone associated with him. He needs to be in the company of friends when he finds out that King is looking for him."

Abby introduced Lucy to Howard at the dinner table and light conversation continued through to dessert. Abby waited until Howard stood to excuse himself from the table and very methodically she said, "Please sit back down Howard, there is something that needs to be discussed."

"You look pretty serious, Abby, what is it?"

Not alluding to what he had done, she simply said, "King knows where you are."

Howard regarded her quizzically for a moment. "King? How do you know about King? I've never mentioned anything about him." A suffocating sensation tightened his throat as the new information twisted and turned inside him. He didn't want to run again but if King knew his whereabouts he wouldn't have a choice. He took a huge risk by leaving King's employment and the penalty for being disloyal would certainly be death.

Raw hurt glittered in his eyes as he stared at Abby. "I guess I need to be saying goodbye. If he knows where I am, it won't be long 'til he shows his face. I don't want to put any of you in danger. You still didn't tell me how you know this."

"That's not real important right now but what is important is that we keep you safe."

Howard interrupted, "You don't understand. There is no safe place to hide from King. He has eyes in every corner of the world. How else would he have uncovered me?"

"He hired someone to find you and lucky for you, the man has a conscience. He knew what King had planned and decided to help you. Now, we just have to find a way to keep you safe."

A hot wave of shame, unexpected and unwanted, washed over him as he stared silently at this woman. He cleared his throat and spoke. "I appreciate your concern Abby, but this is my battle and I will not bring all of you into the combat zone." His words seemed to be falling out painfully from between tightly clenched teeth. "You have no idea what King is capable of. I'm ashamed to say but I've seen the hurt he's caused to people who have gotten in his way. And when his right-hand man goes rogue, you can bet he'll do whatever he has to, to get me back where he thinks I belong. He hates betrayal."

Abby took charge with quiet assurance. "We will not let anything happen to you, Howard. I'm calling Tim, the Chief of Police, and inform him of the situation. He and his men can be on the lookout for such a character as King. New Hope doesn't see many men like Kingsley Spencer. According to Lucy's description, I think he'll stand out like a sore thumb. If he arrives, trust me, he won't be able to hide."

The tension was obvious in Howard's attitude, but watching Abby's face gave him some peace. He knew she and Harley would do all they could to protect him and still continue with their everyday routine. It was probably an understatement to say that he had brought some anxiety into their lives.

CHAPTER 21

Let all that you do be done in love.

1 Corinthians 16:14

Lilly looked out the window and saw Shirley and Abby coming down the sidewalk. She hoped they were coming in for lunch. She watched them open the door and motioned for them to sit in the far corner booth. She had some mighty important information to share during her break.

"Hi Lilly, how are you?" Abby leaned back against the brown leather booth as she ordered her and Shirley's customary soup and salad. Lilly seemed more distracted than usual today and Abby wondered if it had something to do with her upcoming wedding. As soon as Lilly served the ladies their food, she scooted in beside Abby, all loose-limbed but graceful. She flashed a smile to Abby and said, "I understand you talked to Chief McDonald?" She crossed her arms and raised an amused eyebrow. "Well guess what? He wants me to be a spy. Can you imagine that?"

Abby's eyes squinted with amusement. "A spy? You mean like an undercover agent?"

Lilly could hardly sit still. "Yeah, I didn't think I could get any more excited than I am about the wedding, but after this, maybe I could become one of Charlie's Angels!"

"I wouldn't get that excited if I were you. You could be in real jeopardy here so you need to be sensible and not get caught up in the drama. This man, King, is no one to mess with. I don't know what Chief McDonald has asked you to do, but I know he would never want you to be in any danger."

Lilly let out a short laugh and shook her head. "Don't worry, I find out a lot of information without people even knowing that I'm listening." She smiled as she remembered a past incident. "Have you forgotten how I overheard Joan and Martha discussing their plot for Summer Rain?"

"Yes Lilly, we remember, but we weren't dealing with a dangerous character like King." She closed her hand over Lilly's and said, "We love you, Lilly. We don't want to steal your thunder, we just want you to be safe."

Tears flooded Lilly's eyes. Had she finally found a place where she was wanted and needed? She waited, to find out if Abby was going to retract her statement.

"Lilly, are you okay? Are you crying?"

Even before Abby finished her sentence, Lilly blurted out, "Did you just say you love me?"

"Well, of course we love you."

Lilly wanted to lean into the safety of Abby's assurances, but hearing that someone besides Warren actually loved her was unimaginable to her. No one had ever loved Lilly Fisher. She could still hear her mother's words, "You're just a by-product of a one-night stand." For many years she never knew what that meant until a classmate explained it to her. When she heard the details, she became an infinitely sorrowful spirit, with no one to depend on and no one to defend her. Tainted by the stain of her illegitimate birth, she became an unwanted, unasked-for responsibility. Yet somewhere in the gene pool she received a mixture of tenderness and lethal determination that allowed her to learn how to distance herself from humiliation and pain. She taught herself how to manage diversity and how to be responsible for her own development. The fantasies that made her life bearable were now coming true and she must embrace them with all her ability. Being loved by everyone at Summer Rain was definitely causing a change within her.

With an edge of excitement to her voice, Abby said, "Loving you is a good thing, Lilly. I think it would be unanimous to say that it's one of the easiest things we've ever done! Do you not believe me?"

"I want to believe you, but no one, with the exception of Warren, has ever said that to me before."

Abby and Shirley both felt like crying but, for Lilly's sake, they held it together. Shirley took a deep breath, changed the subject, and said, "Why don't you and Warren come out to the Inn tonight for dinner and we'll wrap up the rest of the wedding details. There's only a few days left 'til the big event and we want to make sure we are ready."

"Thank you, ladies, we'll be there." Lilly slid out of the booth, forgetting her original intention to reveal more of her James Bond assignment, and walked straight to the coffee pot and served her customers.

CHAPTER 22

"Be completely humble and gentle; be patient, bearing with one another in love. Make every effort to keep the unity of the spirit through the bond of peace."

Ephesians 4:2-3

Lilly, Warren and Hoafie arrived at the Inn just as Shirley was taking the roast out of the oven. Hoafie ate so many mashed potatoes, they all joked about how he must have a hollow leg. Even though he didn't understand what they meant, he still rocked with the laughter of his friends.

Abby brought out the wedding planner notebook and went over everything that was already in place and gave Lilly and Warren a chance to add or change any designs. They were both smiling ear to ear, giving Abby the notion they were happy with the existing arrangements.

"Two days, you two, and then you'll be Mr. and Mrs. Warren Wright." The very air around them seemed electrified and Abby saw Lilly's cheeks color under the heat of Warren's gaze and she smiled in approval. How wonderful to see two people so in love.

Harley was going to be glad when this wedding was over. He had never taken more orders or worked so hard in all his life. Not that he minded helping his friends, but he just didn't realize how much preparation went into a twenty-minute ceremony. He had married many couples since he became a minister, but all he had to do was show up and make sure the couple said "I do." Being involved with this part of the wedding gave him a new appreciation for wedding planners.

The day of the wedding, dawn broke from the horizon and brought the promise of a perfect day to Summer Rain. The afternoon sun created a magic aura to the gardens as it glistened off the oyster white gazebo. The white marshmallow clouds drifted lazily under a turquoise sky. A hawk scrolled the updrafts, precisely and persistently as if it wanted to be a part of the celebration.

Harley had planted a medley of wildflowers around the bottom of the lattice work as a surprise for Lilly, since she couldn't decide which kind of flowers she wanted for her wedding.

He was coming from behind the shed when he noticed Abby and Shirley fussing with the table decorations. He watched as the two women positioned and repositioned the centerpieces and straightened the napkins. He grinned and straightened his shoulders, ready to continue his list of chores. In a few hours, he would be dressed in a tux, standing in front of Lilly and Warren asking them to pledge their love to each other. He could think of nothing that would make him happier than joining these two wonderful people together.

He really wasn't trying to hide from Abby but if she saw him he knew there would be questions to answer. Too late. She was waving her arms, gesturing for him to come toward her. "Is everything ready, Harley? When are you getting dressed? Did you remember to get the ice?"

"Not quite, soon and yes."

A warning cloud descended on Abby's face. "Harley don't you play games with me on such an important day. I need things to be perfect."

He grinned mischievously and brushed his lips against hers. "I just gave you my answers to your questions. I'm off to finish my list and the next time I see you should be at the gazebo." He waved goodbye and disappeared around the corner.

Lilly had arrived at the Inn and was standing in front of the mirror, looking at someone she didn't know. Life had been quite chaotic for the past six months and she forgot what it was like to just stand still and take in the moment. Her reflection in the mirror reminded her of her childhood dreams of being a bride. She remembered the discarded onion bag she converted into a make-believe veil and the white tablecloth that functioned as a wedding gown. She had walked through the kitchen, her pretend aisle, so many times there was a path worn on the linoleum. But now she stood here with a real dress and a real matching veil. There was no one to make fun of her or demand that she take it off and get to work.

Shirley and Abby were admiring the beautiful young woman as she remained motionless at the mirror. They watched her facial expressions go from heart-rending to a smile and finally to the most peaceful look they had ever seen. It was wonderful to see someone so happy.

"We hate to interrupt your ponderings, Lilly, but it's almost time to walk down the path."

Lilly turned with a start when Abby touched her arm. She had been so absorbed in reflections of her life that she completely forgot where she was. "I'm ready. How do I look?"

"You look beautiful, Lilly. Warren's liable to pee his pants!"

"Shirley! Don't make me laugh. My mascara will run."

As Abby and Shirley escorted Lilly down the steps toward the gazebo, Abby wondered if someday soon she might be following these same footsteps. She took note of Lilly's vintage, trumpet style, strapless, floor-length gown of pearl white organdy. The natural waistline was emphasized with a peach tinted bow knot. Ruffles, embellished with hand embroidered pale peach flowers, tumbled from mid-thigh to the bottom of the sweep style train. Her headpiece was simply a small veil made of tulle, lace and a peach colored rose. She carried a bouquet of white and peach roses tied with satin streamers, holding showers of sweet alyssum. Abby thought she had never seen a more stunning bride.

They stood, just inside the garden gate, waiting, while a few of the guests found their seats. Warren, Harley and the best man, Hoafie, were already in position. The groom looked a bit anxious while Hoafie's constant animation of happiness prompted smiles on everyone's face. Abby took her place on the opposite side of Hoafie as Lilly's Maid of Honor. When the violinist began playing the traditional wedding march, all eyes watched Lilly as she walked through the gate. Warren was awe-stricken. Never in his life had he seen anyone so beautiful. A single tear rolled down his cheek as he struggled for composure. He was already teary-eyed, how in the world was he going to make it through the vows. She was coming toward him; walking with such grace and elegance, just like in the movies.

He didn't know much about wedding dresses but this was one like he never saw before. But then, Lilly was like no one he ever knew before, so the dress was perfect for her. And she was perfect for him.

Lilly now stood beside Warren, who was oblivious to anyone but this beautiful woman.

Harley, smiling, knowing that if ever there were two people who deserved this much happiness it was these two. Lilly was smiling and radiant. Warren smiling, seduced Lilly with his eyes, causing her hormones to do an excited little dance.

Harley began his traditional homily and eventually drifted into the personal segment about Lilly and Warren. "Lilly serves a mean cup of coffee and she was one of the few who believed in me during my difficult time. She kept me from giving up." He exchanged a smile with her and then looked at Warren. "This guy found himself in a difficult situation, too, when he was being accused of a wrongdoing." A rush of bitter memories pushed down on him and he had to take a minute to recover. By this time, sniffles were heard from the guests and Lilly felt a tear slide down her cheek.

"Abby introduced Warren and me, hoping that my vocation and my life experiences would be able to help, but in the end, I think it was he who helped me. He and Lilly are both strong individuals with hearts of gold. I am so proud to be able to unite them together, today and forever."

Harley leaned over and whispered in Hoafie's ear, asking for the rings. As quickly as he could, Hoafie put the rings in his friend's hand and began clapping. It was infectious and soon everyone joined in. When the applause ended, Harley continued, "Warren and Lilly have each written their own vows and it will be our pleasure to witness evidence of such love. Warren, I'll ask you to go first."

"Lilly, in a short time we have gone through so many good times, bad times, and even scary times. Nevertheless, we are still standing by each other's side. Life will lead us to new paths and challenges but my hand will always be in yours. I promise to tell you that I love you, I miss you, and how beautiful you are to me every day. I want to be the fire in your heart, the laughter of your smile, and the support in your soul. We may seem crazy to everyone else and they could be right, but what we share,

I wouldn't want with anyone else. You are my best friend and soul mate and the one I want to share my life with. I love you."

"Warren, with my whole heart, I take you as my husband, acknowledging and accepting your faults and your strengths, as you do mine. You know me better than most anyone in the world, and somehow you still manage to love me. You are my best friend, my partner in crime, and my one true love. You make me happier than I could have ever imagined, and more loved that I ever thought possible. I am truly blessed to be a part of your life, which, as of today, becomes our life together. There are still times when I can't believe that I'm the one who gets to marry you here today. I promise to be faithful to you, and to make our love my priority. I will be yours in sickness and in health, in failure and in triumph. I promise to dream big with you, celebrate with you, and walk side-by-side with you through whatever our life together brings. These vows are not promises, but privileges. I get to laugh and cry with you, care for you and share with you. You are my person – my love and my life, today, tomorrow, and always."

Overwhelming silence for the next few seconds took over the ceremony until the retrieving of tissues interrupted the quiet. Throughout the crowd, tears were flowing freely and even Harley had to take a minute to compose himself. When he spoke again, his voice reflected happiness. "Without further ado, I now pronounce you husband and wife."

Warren and Lilly shared a smile and without waiting for Harley's announcement to kiss the bride, Warren captured Lilly's mouth in a kiss that made her head reel. The guests began cheering and applauding the new couple, anxious to congratulate them.

Harley had to shout over the crowd's noise, but he happily announced, "I now give you Mr. and Mrs. Warren Wright."

The electric orange of the summer night only added to the ambiance of the evening. Slaps on the back and hugs set the tone for everyone. The guests seemed to bond quickly with each other and the gathering felt more like a family reunion than a wedding reception.

When the late hour finally convinced the guests to go home, Lilly and Warren collapsed into the nearest chairs. Even though they were exhausted, they felt sad to have the evening end. A wonderful sense of going home began filling their minds and their hearts. Neither had ever thought of home as some place they wanted to be, but it was now taking on a whole new meaning. Lilly pressed a hand to her chest and batted her lashes at Warren, "This has been the most wonderful day of my life, but I'm ready to go home."

Warren murmured in a very captivating voice, "Whatever you say Mrs. Warren Wright. I, too, am ready to leave this place and begin our new life together as husband and wife." Within minutes they were waving goodbye and running to the car.

Since Hoafie would be spending the night at the Inn, Howard helped to get him up from the bench where he had fallen asleep, and escort him upstairs. The leftover food was carried in and lights were turned off. It was the end of an absolutely perfect day.

CHAPTER 23

The sacrifice of the wicked is an abomination;
how much more when he brings it with evil intent.

Proverbs 21:27

Trying to keep a low profile, King rented a mid-size car to visit the town of New Hope. His black Mercedes would attract too much attention. Normally he would have his henchman find and return Howard, but he had come to think of the young man as a son. He needed to pursue this hunt on his own. What could possibly have caused him to run? Did it have something to do with his mother? Never in a million years would King have believed his protégé would leave him in the lurch. And yet, he had spent the last ten hours on a plane just to get to this location. That was the easy part. Now he had to figure out how to maneuver around this one-horse town without causing suspicions. There was a sign for a diner up ahead and he remembered he hadn't eaten since last night. Diners usually displayed a welcome mat for travelers, hence not drawing attention to a stranger. As he parked the car, he could already smell sausage and bacon frying. His stomach let out a loud moan just as he opened the glass door. He found a seat right inside the door, where he could see everyone coming and going. Who knew? He might get lucky and get a glimpse of Howard.

"Good morning sir, can I get you a cup of coffee?"

Lilly felt the burn of the stranger's gaze as it fixed on hers. He lit a cigarette and eyed her through the flame of the match.

"I'm sorry sir, but smoking is not allowed in the diner."

"Is that so? Well, for you pretty lady, I'll put it out. Now, how about that cup of coffee? I like it black."

Lilly's legs felt leaden as she moved toward the coffee pot. She quickly poured the black liquid, returned to the stranger's table and asked if he would like to see a menu.

"No, I just want one of those fluffy omelets that's advertised on the sign, and some rye toast."

Lilly's hands were shaking so bad she could hardly write the order. A creeping uneasiness at the bottom of her heart told her this had to be King. He was exactly as Howard described him. She thanked him, put in the order and rushed to the restroom. She had to pull herself together if she were going to get any information. James Bond would not be associated with a secret agent who couldn't get to first base. She wanted to help Howard but she especially wanted Warren to be proud of her. Maybe she could have a career as a detective. Agent Lilly Wright, it did have a nice ring to it. Who was she kidding? She was Warren's wife now and that was all she needed to be.

Eavesdropping was something Lilly had learned to do very well without anyone even knowing. Most times the information caused her to chuckle, but this time it would help Howard if she could extract information from King. When she returned with his food, the stranger was talking angrily on a mobile phone, warning the person on the other end about not receiving pay if the job wasn't finished. "Like they say, Lou, if you want something done right, you gotta' do it yourself. Yea, I'm looking for him and I promise I will find him." With that, he ended the call and watched Lilly's backside as she wiped down the table and chairs next to him.

Nonchalantly, Lilly walked to the kitchen and dialed the police station, all the while watching the outsider. While relating the information to the Chief, Lilly saw King abruptly stand up and walk out the door. Lilly's spitfire tongue told Tim all he needed to know.

The plain-clothed deputy was across the street, sitting on a bench reading the newspaper, when he saw King emerge from the diner. He waited until King drove away before he jumped in his car and began following him. He was shocked when he saw him turn into the Holiday

Inn. The deputy drove around the block and parked where he could see King as he got out of his car. He radioed Tim with the information. "We can't arrest him for stopping at a hotel but I want twenty-four-hour surveillance on him. He's dangerous and I want to know his every move."

Tim called Harley right away and informed him of King's whereabouts. "Lilly didn't get much information from King but she did find out that he's looking for someone. I'm hoping he will visit the diner again and she can be a bit friendlier. Other than shadowing him, she's our only go-between."

Even though using Lilly as a spy could be dangerous, it brought hope toward apprehending King. A good-humored grin took over Tim's face as he said, "Let's hope he gets hungry again real soon."

Chapter 24

And he said to him, "Truly, I say to you, today you will be with me in Paradise.

Luke 23:43

Howard rolled slowly off his pillow, leaned toward the nightstand and picked up his watch. He couldn't believe he slept this late. Since living here, he had no need for an alarm clock. The smell of bacon frying every morning was as certain as the sunrise and always brought his feet to the floor without hesitation. This was the first morning that, even with extra attempts of sucking in air through his nose, his room was lacking that comforting smell. Where could everyone be? He grabbed his robe and headed down the stairs. He checked the kitchen and the sunroom – no one was to be found. Another suggestion that something was wrong. This house was never empty. Panicking, he decided to get dressed and check outside. Maybe everyone was on early clean-up duty from last night's event. But as he began his climb up the stairs, a sleepy-eyed Shirley emerged from her bedroom. "Good morning Howard. You're up early!"

"I am? Where is everyone? I was just ready to go searching outside."

"What's the matter? Shirley's lips twitched in amusement. "Miss the smell of bacon, don't you?"

Just like this woman he thought of as a mother, to make him smile in the middle of his uneasiness. "A little bit yes, but I was more concerned when I couldn't find anyone."

"This is a rarity, but we all slept in this morning. The past two weeks have obviously taken a toll, especially on this old body." Shirley moved toward the stairs but stopped short of the first step. Suddenly her jaw tightened, screaming for release. Her left arm froze like it was suddenly thrust inside an iceberg. With her right hand, she reached for Howard's arm. By this time, he realized something was terribly wrong. He bellowed, "Help" as he lowered Shirley to the floor. He cradled her head in his trembling hands while her chest began heaving laboriously. She closed her eyes while she tried to draw in a slow, calming breath but the pain was too much. Lines of strain around her mouth were deepening and the pressure she felt squeezing her windpipe, made it impossible to speak. Even though she tried, only a groan passed from her lips. A flicker of a smile rose at the edges of her mouth, then died out.

The instant Abby saw Shirley on the floor she became hysterical.

"Howard, what happened?"

"I don't know, but hurry and call 911. It's probably another heart attack. Get me a blanket, too. She's freezing cold."

Howard began hearing a myriad of sounds --voices, murmurs and unbelievably loud sirens, their frequencies plucking at the nerves in his head. The unfamiliar voices were telling him to move aside and allow them to work. He stood up and pushed his hands deep into his pockets, not knowing what else to do. He watched as the medical team quickly administered thrombolysis medicine through an IV in her arm, while aggressively placing a nitroglycerin pill under her tongue. Shirley's heart went into sudden shock and the youngest of the team went to work, giving heart compressions, trying desperately to jolt her back to life. The beeping on the machines went back to normal and everyone breathed a sigh of relief. She was quickly laid on the gurney and rolled to the ambulance. Abby's mind began remembering this very same scenario, not all that long ago. She began praying that the outcome would be the same and Shirley would come back home. She couldn't imagine life without this wonderful woman.

Harley was on his way to the Inn when he heard the siren before he saw the source. His heart nearly jumped out the window as he noted Abby's car following the ambulance. He slammed on the brakes, turned in the middle of the road and followed the two speeding vehicles. Assuming Shirley was the patient, he began an intense prayer. If Shirley didn't make it, there would not only be an empty chair at meal time, but Abby's heart would be overcome with sadness. He knew how much she loved and respected Shirley and losing her would be devastating.

He caught up with Abby, just as she was jumping out of her car and racing through the emergency room doors. Once inside, she stopped to catch her breath and realized that the medical team was no longer in a hurry. Being in this environment, the smells and constant beeping, opened the doors to memories she tried to bury. Why had they stopped rushing? Every minute counted with heart attack victims. She grabbed a medic by the sleeve and shook him as hard as she could, all the while screaming at him to help Shirley. Harley sprinted towards Abby, his hand landing in the middle of her back, anchoring her against him. She tried to wiggle free but was halted by an iron grip on her wrist. Harley was surprised at her strength as she pulled her hand free of his. "Abby, please. You know why they're not hurrying. They did all they could but Shirley's gone. You need to calm down if you want to be able to see her one last time and say your goodbyes."

As the tears of reality fell, Abby was pushing words across to Harley. "Why Harley? Why would God take this woman away from so many people who need her? Why does he keep taking the people I love away from me?" Struggling to keep the desperation out of her voice, she clenched her teeth against the wave of hopeless, bitter pain. "Is God punishing me for something?"

"No Abby, it was just Shirley's time to go home with the Lord. I loved her too, and even though you had a special bond with her, she's going to be missed by *everyone*. I understand your anger and all the questions, but she didn't have the quality of life this past year, that she truly wanted. Her activities were so limited and I think she was more tired than she ever let us know."

Harley took both of her hands in his and calmly said, "Shirley's doctor is waiting for you in the room across the hall. There are a few papers that need to be signed; she had you listed as next of kin."

The memories of "paper signing" came crowding back, like a hidden current, ready to wash her out to sea. She *could* not and *would* not do this again. She felt unexpectedly trapped by the memory of her own emotions.

How would she ever find her way out of this upheaval in her life? A cold shiver spread over her as she remembered the aftermath of her husband's death. The days seemed like weeks and the weeks felt like months. The emotional pain actually caused physical pain and she weakened in the silence that engulfed her. It was that hungering for attachment that had compelled her to return to work. It was there that a friend introduced her to the white house with the front porch – Summer Rain - the house that stimulated her recovery and introduced her to the next chapter of her life. Shirley had been the most influential person in her life after Jeff's death. She helped Abby with the grieving process and gave her opportunity to bring light back into her life. And now – now that light would never shine again. Shirley's absence would surely cause darkness.

Harley's voice broke into her thoughts. "Abby, they are waiting for your signature but it's not for what you think." Abby's eyes darkened with pain and Harley felt helpless as he continued. "They are not asking for Shirley's organs. These are not donor permits. It's only a release form to the funeral home."

She looked up at him with what he knew to be quiet strength and simply said, "Thank you." She reluctantly stood from her chair and walked across the hall to sign papers that would once again take away a loved one.

Returning home was harder than the previous time because Abby knew that Shirley would never again grace Summer Rain with her presence. The house was already exuding an awareness that seemed to blanket the air with sadness. She imagined the flowers drooping on the wallpaper and the curtains waiting to fall from the windows.

Shirley had been such a force in this house that Abby didn't know if the ambiance would ever be the same. She didn't know if *she* would ever be the same.

CHAPTER 25

"He will wipe away every tear from their eyes, and death shall be no more," neither shall there be mourning, nor crying, nor pain anymore, for the former things have passed away."

Revelation 21:4

As it did every morning, the crimson globe rose from behind the mountains with the promise of another wonderful day. Abby's eyes were so clouded with sorrow, she swore the sun appeared even redder, just like it, too, had cried all night. The entire house seemed surrounded with silence, especially in the kitchen, the room where Shirley spent so much time, cooking and baking, taking care of her family.

Abby meandered through the house, smiling with remembered pleasure, the memories so vivid, so clear. She remembered the day she walked up the steps to the big wrap-around porch anticipating her meeting with Shirley. Little did she know how much her life would be impacted with this woman of faith. Shirley offered her something she hadn't felt in a long time– a mother's love. Abby was only five years old when her mother passed, and she had very little memory of her. Her past was soon forgotten as she became smothered under the blanket of Shirley's love. Shirley had taught her how to live in the present and to be grateful for what she had now, not what she lost. Before meeting Shirley, she took so much for granted. She sincerely felt that it was now her purpose in life to pass this wisdom on to her friends and family.

Abby knew sadness would fill this house for a long time but if she practiced the wisdom Shirley exhibited, maybe she could turn the shadows of grief into threads of light. She wanted everyone to feel

Shirley's presence always, and by doing that, happiness and aspirations of hope must be maintained in the Summer Rain household, even without Shirley. She found herself going up the stairs and walking toward Shirley's bedroom. Shades of green and the scent of 'Moonlight,' Shirley's perfume, surrounded her as she stood just inside the doorway. She wanted to turn around and walk out, never to enter this room again, but it was as if Shirley herself were inside pulling on her heart strings, coaxing her to come sit on the bed and visit awhile. There was no one to talk to or even to say goodnight. The only thing she could say was' goodbye' and she just wasn't ready for that yet.

Harley called out to Abby as he opened the back door, "Anyone home? Abby, are you here?"

Eyes swollen and red from crying, she answered him with only a whisper, "I'm up here." When he found her, she was sitting on the floor, leaning against Shirley's chair. He knelt down and began kneading her stiff muscles with both hands. What he really wanted to do was pull Abby into his arms and soothe away all the pain she was feeling, but he was feeling it too. And who was going to help him? Abby could barely hold herself together, let alone comfort him. He rubbed his forehead as he silently asked God to once again give him the right words during a difficult situation. How were they all going to survive without the woman known as 'Mom'? Everyone who belonged to this household had come to think of Shirley as a necessary part of life, like air and water.

Harley remained silent as he finally took Abby in his arms and simply held her close to him. He just prayed that God would give him the perfect words to say but silence seemed to be golden right now. He learned in the past that, sometimes, God's wisdom included stillness. He held her until she fell asleep, picked her up and carried her to her bedroom. He retrieved a blanket from Shirley's bed, knowing that covering Abby with her mother's love could only enhance her rest. He went back down the stairs hoping to find some rest for himself, but instead found Howard brewing coffee and crying like a baby.

Howard's despondent frown flitted across his features similar to the bats wings in the cave. The minute he saw Harley, he jumped up from his chair and turned away. There was no way he was going to let Harley see a strong man, such as himself, crying like a babbling idiot. He swiped at the tears with the pads of his thumbs, but it was too late. His dark eyes were already showing signs of the tortured dullness of disbelief. Disbelief that Shirley would no longer grace this house with her presence. She had made a big impression on Howard, and Harley was sure she also touched the stranger's inner being. Even though Howard only knew her for a short time, he loved her, and he felt her love for him. Having those feelings was a whole new experience for Howard and he hadn't been ready to admit it. Now that Shirley would no longer be here to encourage him, his insecurities were resurfacing again. Emotions had no history for Howard and now not only feeling emotional pain, physical pain was running down his cheeks. He realized in these past few months he had more options in life than being a prisoner of money and drugs.

Harley still didn't know everything about Howard, especially his childhood, but seeing this more tender side of him, made Harley smile.

With no expression on his face, Howard asked, "Harley, what are you smiling about?"

"I just can't help it, Howard. Seeing what I just saw would make Shirley so happy. Even though they are tears of grief, it *is* an emotion. Something you're not used to dealing with. You've lived so long with anger and resentment about your mother you've never allowed yourself to feel love or any of the *good* emotions. Shirley obviously broke through that wall of fear and gave you an opportunity to see other ways of life and to learn that not everyone is against you. It's not about the waterworks I saw on your face, but about the rejoicing in your heart. Shirley knew deep down inside you are a good man, Howard, and if her dying made you see that, then she is in heaven celebrating. She's crying too, only hers are tears of joy. It's okay to cry Howard, and we're all going to miss her and we wanted her to be part of this family forever but we know that's not possible. Be happy, Howard that you were part of her purpose here on earth."

Harley spoke while Howard remained silent. "She allowed Abby and me to be part of her life, giving it more meaning, just as she allowed you to be like a son to her. She would be happy to know you loved her too. I need you to help me show Abby how we need to celebrate her life, not agonize over her death. She's with the Lord now and she's in no more pain. That alone calls for smiles. I can't imagine life around here without her, but remember, some of our best living is done through the people we leave behind. Shirley may have left us in the wake, but she's still always one step in front of us. Let's continue in her footsteps and embrace her purpose here on earth."

Howard knew the deck had been stacked against him since the day he was born and he learned early in life not to care, to never expect anything from anyone – until he met Shirley. Caring came so easy for her. She just took him in, like a bird in a shoebox, no questions asked. He knew she wanted to know about his background but he held her at bay and now, when he wanted to tell her, she was gone. He wanted to react like the preacher man was telling him, but the hurt was just too raw.

"I appreciate you trying to make me feel better, Harley and as I'm sure you know, I'm not a cryin' man. I just never knew what it was like to be a part of a family 'til I met Shirley. Why did she have to go and die? I needed her. You talk about your God and how great he is, but why would he take a woman like Shirley and leave scum like me to continue living?" He cut Harley a sharp look that dared him to argue. "How do you make sense of that preacher man?"

"I don't make sense of it Howard, I just live by faith. God has a plan and who am I to rearrange his strategy? That's why He's God. I really don't want any more responsibility. I have to trust that He needs you on this earth more than He needed Shirley. Her work was obviously done and you clearly are supposed to promenade in her footsteps. You can shake your fists or bend your knees – it's totally up to you how you handle your life from here on out. I'm not a gambling man but I'm betting that we are going to see some phenomenal inspirations from you in the future."

Howard reluctantly pushed away from the counter and looked down into his coffee cup seemingly expecting all the answers to his questions to be printed there. Why *had* God brought him to Summer Rain? Was he really part of a plan he didn't know about?

A cold shiver spread over him as a flash brought to mind another man who also had a plan for his future. And he too, was called 'King.' The flash was so strong, for a fractured second, he was thrown back in time. In all fairness, Kingsley Spencer had taken care of him, treated him as a son and provided him with a pretty good life, but with all that, came a price. As a father bonds with his son, King slowly merged Howard into the domain of criminal activity. As Howard became more and more familiar with corrupt behavior, his shrewd practices provided him with not only a luxurious lifestyle but also a great reputation for himself in the world controlled by King. It was the first time in his life he ever made someone proud. And he had to admit that he liked the feeling. Finding out about his mother, though, had generated a new feeling. It was then he began to recognize his true needs. He was craving love. He wanted to give real love. He needed to believe that his mother loved him. He needed to know why she allowed him to be raised in foster homes. And when she lay on her death bed, his heart longed to see her one more time.

Even though his mother gave him no answers about her love or the foster home, she had, in the last few moments of her fatal condition, reached out and offered him a chance to love his brother. He had sensed love at a far distance, never daring to approach it, but resisting reality and attempting the needle in a haystack search had brought him to Summer Rain. So, even if he never found the love of his brother, he had found Shirley. She opened his heart to more love than he ever thought possible for him. And was all of that by chance or had God developed a plan for his life from the very beginning? Preacher Man believed in all that Bible stuff but it was something Howard knew nothing about. Pride had kept him from asking, even though he wanted whatever it was this household exhibited.

Abby's voice was soft and eminently reasonable, "Hi Howard, are you okay? You look quite shattered, as we all are. I'm just not sure I'm going to be able to survive without Shirley. She was my rock. She always knew just what to say to make me feel better." Abby's face tightened at the use of the past tense and tears rolled down her cheeks.

Howard gave Abby a sympathetic hug and with his voice vibrating, he said, "Well, I am sure not Shirley 'cause I don't know what to say to make you feel better, but I do know she wouldn't want you to be sad. From what I've been hearing, you brought a lot of joy into her life. You allowed her to stay in her home and she trusted you. She told me how happy she was when you asked if you could call her 'Mom.' Even though your name is on the deed to this property, you respected her ways and her wisdom. You made her an integral part of Summer Rain and you made her last years happy ones. She loved you, Abby. The way Preacher Man talks about heaven, you should be glad you know she's there, happy and reunited with her husband. Isn't that how it all works?"

Abby's voice was choked with sincerity, "That's quite a speech for you, Howard. And you said you didn't know how to make me feel better!"

"Really? I made you feel better?"

"Don't get me wrong, I'm going to miss her. I already do, but I hadn't thought about the reunion with her husband. I know how much she missed him."

Already reaching for a tea cup, Howard smiled, "Let me do something for you that I learned from Shirley. She taught me how to make a mean cup of tea."

"That was one of her comforting techniques. She believed in always having a cup of tea near. It's a good tradition to carry on through the decades, don't you think?"

"I think anything that woman did was worth doing or believing. I wish I could have known her longer, but I'm grateful for the time I had. She gave me hope for my future."

Howard was a bit uncomfortable talking about things he only pretended to know, so when Abby answered the ringing phone he quietly left the room. It was Mr. Peabody, the funeral director. "Good afternoon Ms. Weaver. I'm calling to set up a time for you to come make the arrangements for Shirley Black. You were listed as next of kin."

A voice cut the silence. "Hello, Ms. Weaver. Are you still there? Hello?

"Yes Mr. Peabody, I'm still here, I just don't want to do what you're asking."

"I understand, but the celebration of Mrs. Black's life can't happen unless you help me. I knew Shirley and she was a wonderful person. I want nothing more than to provide her with a great service. I know that's what you want for her too, so if you could come in this afternoon we could start the planning."

Abby called Harley and asked him to meet her at the funeral home. Even with him by her side, she wasn't sure she could get through this.

Memories of Jeff's funeral came flooding back. Her face burned as she allowed the subconscious to surface. Now wasn't the day to pick up the strings of time and recall the music, the crying and especially the final goodbye. She needed to remember they were celebrating Shirley's life, not regretting it.

A few more uncontrollable tears fell as she pulled into the parking lot but she wiped them dry and entered the building. She knew Shirley was waiting for her, in spirit, and she dare not be late.

Harley was waiting for her and together they planned a celebration to honor their beloved Shirley.

CHAPTER 26

*For judgment is without mercy to one who has shown
no mercy. Mercy triumphs over judgment.*

James 2:13

Life as everyone knew it at Summer Rain was no longer the same. No
smell of bacon frying in the morning, the tea kettle didn't whistle
as much and the evidence of a baker's presence no longer lingered in the
kitchen. Meals were relatively bland compared to the Inn's reputation
and conversations were not quite as lighthearted as they had been with
Shirley at the table.

Abby needed a chef. New Hope was a town filled with mom
and pop diners, not exquisite restaurants employing high end cooks,
so hiring someone with a broader variety of cuisine was presenting a
problem. Everyone was sharing the load of responsibilities that Shirley
so graciously performed, but the Inn was now very seldom empty and
even the routine chores were becoming a challenge.

Howard overheard Abby on the phone talking to an ad agency about
hiring a chef and possibly an assistant. He waited until she was finished
talking and asked exactly what the responsibilities would be for the
person she hired.

"Why are you asking, Howard? Do you know someone that's qualified?"

"Maybe."

"Could you contact them and see if they are interested?"

"Oh, he would be interested but he has a criminal background and he
wouldn't want the Inn to get a reputation of that sort."

Abby sucked her mouth into a rosette and said, "Since when do we judge people here at Summer Rain? We're all here because of second chances. If this person has your blessing, and he's qualified, he can start tomorrow. What's his name?" Abby dismissed him with a casual wave while her voice rang with command, "Go give him a call right now!"

Howard sighed, then slipped his hands into his pockets and without looking directly at Abby said, "His name is Howard."

"You have a friend named Howard? What're the chances of that happening? Obviously, he doesn't live around here. If he takes the job, how long will it take him to get here?"

"Slow down Abby. I know this guy quite well and he could start cooking tomorrow." Howard began explaining, with modesty. "Spencer Kingsley gave me a choice to go to school for whatever I wanted as long as I continued my night work at the casinos. I grew up constantly hungry. Every household I ever lived in was always short on food. I vowed and declared that as an adult, my cupboards would be full. Therefore, I chose culinary school and found that I was actually quite good. I was offered jobs at classy restaurants but King would not allow me to pursue a career. The years I spent in school was a way to control me and keep me within the boundaries of his rules."

Dust was the only movement in the kitchen as Abby stood staring at Howard, like an animal looking out from the brush. There was a long, silent, sizing-up moment before she recognized a spark of emotion in his eyes. As he talked about culinary school they seemed to shine with excitement.

Abby simply shook her head. "I must say, Howard, you sure are a man of many surprises. I've never seen any indication, in all these months, that you had the slightest interest in the kitchen. Maybe you should try out for Broadway!"

"It's not that I am so good at acting, it's just that it was a dream I knew was never going to happen and so I put it as far back in my mind as possible. I felt delusional even thinking about it, so I didn't. When you talked about hiring a chef a few minutes ago, it opened a door to a lot of memories I tried to bury. My desire to *help* you surpassed my need to keep a secret. Maybe this could be a way to help pay you back for everything you have done for me." He bowed his head and remained in an attitude of frozen stillness.

Abby was still stunned. How should she respond to his revelation? She was happy he felt confident enough to reveal his secret to her but how many other secrets was he was keeping? How had he been so close to Shirley in the kitchen and never even tried to help her. Was he so desperate now that he was once again acting?

She turned on him with a sudden flash of defensive spirit, "Okay, hot shot, let's see what you can round up for dinner tonight. The kitchen's all yours." Knowing her words were dripping with disrespect, she hurried out of the kitchen and went straight to her bedroom. What had just happened to her? She had no cause to talk to Howard that way. She wasn't usually a cynic, but honesty was part of her makeup. She had just been honest and look how she acted. Challenging him to prove his worth was not a very gracious attitude, especially when he needed to witness true generosity from Abby, who promoted grace every chance she got. Why had she been so unyielding in her hasty judgment? There was only one thing she could do and that was to apologize to Howard.

She edged herself off the bed and went looking for Howard. He was still in the kitchen lingering over his coffee cup. He seemed preoccupied with his thoughts and she contemplated whether to disturb him. What she needed to say was important so she opted to just interrupt him. "Hi Howard. Sorry to intrude into your quiet time, but I think I owe you an apology."

He lifted his head and gave her an I-don't-need-your-pity look but said nothing.

"You know, when you first came here, I was really leery of your intentions, but Shirley had such a strong feeling about you so I dismissed those thoughts and welcomed you into our home. I was even excited about helping you find your brother. You've come to grow on me and everyone involved here at Summer Rain. We're even trying to help with your Kingsley situation. You've given us no reason to think you're a fraud. I'm still reeling over the fact that Shirley is never coming back and when you told me about knowing how to cook, all I could think about was the woman I called 'Mom.' I didn't understand how you could keep such a great talent to yourself, especially when there were many times we could have used your skill. I reacted to the chapter instead of waiting for the entire book. You *did* try to explain it to me but having never walked in your shoes, I missed the significance of your position. I have never lived in foster homes or on the street. I've never been enslaved by a ruthless boss or had my life threatened if I didn't obey. I do know what emotional pain feels like and the older I get the more I realize that not everyone's pain is equal. To me, what you've had to deal with over the years is extremely overwhelming."

Abby could see Howard's defenses slowly melting away, like a snowman in the winter sun. His eyes revealed an intense, clear light of true surrender. A shattered man, ready to relinquish the old for the new.

"I'm sorry I didn't tell you about cooking but I couldn't imagine anyone wanting my help. I've never really been good at anything except countin' cards and stealing people's hard-earned money. I was just more or less a robot for the King. He programmed me and I processed the goods. It's all I knew until I met you folks. You've unleashed something inside of me that I don't understand. When you walked out on me earlier, I knew you were upset but I couldn't figure out why. Cooking was not important where I come from and I saw no reason to even mention it. King made me feel like a mamma's boy, just because I liked to be in the kitchen, so I wasn't about to chance that here in this household, even though deep down I knew you wouldn't do that to me. King calibrated my heart just like a mechanic adjusts a car engine to increase production."

By this time, Abby was crying and for lack of knowing what to do, she threw her arms around Howard and gave him a sisterly hug. She wanted him to know she really was sorry and she couldn't wait to eat dinner tonight. Howard finally smiled and returned the hug.

He snickered and nudged Abby with his elbow, "Dinner's at six. Don't be late. Oh, and don't forget to invite Preacher Man!"

CHAPTER 27

"So, whether you eat or drink, or whatever you do,
do all to the glory of God."

1 Corinthians 10:31

Harley was in total shock when he came into the kitchen and saw Howard standing by the oven with baking mitts on both hands. His first instinct was to laugh but when he saw the serious expression on Howard's face he decided against it. For a moment, Harley forgot that Shirley was gone, as the sweet aroma of baking bread filled his nostrils. Did Howard really think he could come into hallowed ground and fill Shirley's shoes? He must have inhaled too much yeast.

"Good afternoon, Howard. What's going on in the kitchen? Nobody fed you lately so you're trying your hand at cooking?"

"I am. I'm taking care of dinner tonight and since Abby hasn't invited you yet, I'm doing it right now. As I told her, dinner is at six, don't be late."

Harley shot him a good-natured smile and clapped an arm around his shoulders. "What's on the menu, grilled cheese sandwiches?"

With an over-confident smile Howard answered with another question. "Why don't you just show up and find out?"

The rest of the day dragged as Harley anticipated the evening meal. He made sure he was in the dining room before six and waited, expecting sandwiches from a fast food joint. He was flabbergasted when Howard appeared carrying a gold rimmed china platter laden with a crown roast of pork complete with mushroom dressing and roasted vegetables. It was a beautiful sight, one that Harley had never seen. After many oohs and ahs from Abby, Howard smiled and asked Harley to give the blessing.

Conversation was kept light and with everyone's appetite appeased, they retired to the sunroom for a white chocolate mousse topped with strawberries and whipped cream.

"I must say Howard, you've made a believer out of me. I will never again assume what a man can't do until I've seen what he *can* do. That food was amazing. What other talents are you hiding?"

"As I told Abby, I didn't think of it as a talent and no one has ever needed my help before. She can fill you in on the details of this afternoon's conversation." He smiled with an even bigger air of confidence as he left the room. "Since I'm on staff here now, I better finish cleaning up the kitchen."

Harley looked at Abby with questioning eyes. "He's on staff here? Since when?"

Abby said the words cautiously, testing the idea, "Since he proved he can cook."

"One meal doesn't support an entire menu."

"Maybe not, but tonight's meal was wonderful and I have a feeling we've stumbled onto something even Howard didn't know was possible. We need help and for the first time in his life, he feels needed."

Harley settled his elbows on the table and steepled his fingers. An urge to protect her from any more hurt washed over him and he spoke softly, "Abby I love you for your compassion and your big heart. You seem to have a sixth sense about someone in need and you're always ready to catch them when they fall." He stroked her cheek with the back of his knuckles and planted a kiss.

Stunned by his intensity, Abby's heart reacted immediately as tears streamed down her face. A feeling of happiness rose inside her. It had been a long time since she felt so content.

Howard cleared his throat. "You two look like you want to be left alone. Answer one question and I'll be out of your hair." Sweat broke out on Howard's brow as he asked, "Should I plan tomorrow's meals or are you still putting an ad in the paper for a new chef?"

Abby met his steady gaze then quickly glanced at Harley, anticipating an answer.

"I'm on board no matter what you decide."

The magnitude of Abby's smile permeated the air in the sunroom, causing Howard's worry lines to melt away like butter. For the first time in his life, he initiated a hug to another human being. Happiness sprang up in Abby's heart as she received the hug. Surprised and somewhat thrilled by his own behavior, Howard moved his head slightly to establish perspective and then stepped away from Abby. "Thanks Abby and Harley. I promise I won't let you down. If I can borrow your car, I'll be on my way to the grocery store."

"Take it, Howard. Why don't you stop at Freedom's and see if she needs something from the shelves as well. She would probably be happy to see you."

"I think I'll wait till daylight. She's quite skilled with that shotgun of hers and if she's gonna shoot it, I want her to be able to see the target. Hopefully she won't shoot it at me." Howard smiled and hurried out the door.

Abby and Harley said their goodnights and departed into the night. Abby fell asleep dreaming of someday becoming Mrs. Harley Davidson. Harley couldn't sleep thinking about someday becoming a married man.

CHAPTER 28

He is not afraid of bad news; his heart is firm,
trusting in the Lord.

Psalm 112:7

Howard unlocked Abby's car and crawled in behind the steering wheel. He sat there in the dark for a moment, thinking about the past few hours. He realized that, over the years, he had acquired skills but not much wisdom. Living in this household, for only a few months, had definitely improved his common sense. He knew deep down his boss would never quit looking for him, yet months had passed and the danger he imagined following him never showed its face. He was trying very hard to believe Miss Shirley's idea that he was here on this earth for a purpose, that God had a plan for him. It was easier to believe in the Almighty when life was extremely good. Feeling safe and optimistic were new ways of thinking for Howard. His heart truly wanted to believe, but the disparity he had lived with all his life, kept him from absolute trust. He didn't want to be always looking over his shoulder, but without the King's men or King himself showing up in person, he would have no choice. A flicker of his stalker would always be in the shadows.

His thoughts caused him to neglect seeing the car parked on the other side of the road near the driveway. He didn't notice it until its headlights shined too close to his bumper.

The first thud was strong enough to be felt but not hard enough to do damage. However, it was enough to remind Howard that he could never allow himself to be oblivious to his surroundings. He pushed the gas pedal harder, to outrun the car behind him. If he could reach the police station he would have a chance to discourage the driver. As he neared the building he created a disturbance with a constant blare from the horn. He pulled into the parking space and continued the ruckus. The car sped by him, giving him a chance to escape into the police station.

Chief McDonald loaded his pistol and got ready for action. But when he had Howard in his scope, he dropped the gun and rushed to Howard's side, pushing him to the floor, just as the window shattered, flinging shards of glass on top of the two men. He made radio contact with the two sergeants on duty, asking them to put out an all-points bulletin for a gray mini-van.

"Howard, are you all right? What happened? Do you think it's Kings men?"

"There's no one else it could be. He was waiting for me out by the Inn. I have Abby's car though, so how did he know it was me?" A painful expression came across Howard's face. He looked at Tim and said, "He didn't know it was me, did he? That could have been Abby. He's willing to hurt anyone associated with me, isn't he?"

"Looks that way, Howard. You better call Abby and tell her to make sure everything is locked up tight. Who knows how many men we're dealing with. I'll send a patrol car out there just to be doubly sure."

Fear and anger knotted inside Howard. He found the phone on Tim's desk and dialed the Inn. After several rings, Abby answered, and with sharpness in his voice, Howard shouted, "Abby, don't let Harley leave and lock the doors, quick!"

"Howard, is this you? What is wrong?"

"Just do as I say Abby, NOW!"

He heard her drop the phone as she yelled for Harley. Within seconds, Preacher Man picked up the phone and started asking questions.

"No time to talk until everything is locked up and lights are turned off. I'll wait on the phone till you tell me you've done as I said."

Once again, he heard the receiver drop as Harley followed instructions. He soon returned, barely able to speak, a thin thread of mania evident in his voice. "Okay Howard, what is going on? Where are you and should we leave? Thankfully, Abby and I are the only ones here tonight." In a tone of voice one might use to reprimand a dog, Harley said "speak."

"I'm with the Chief. Someone tried to run me off the road and then they took a shot at me here at the Chief's office. I'm sure it's King or one of his men. The police are on alert and a patrol car should already be at the Inn. Do not go outside or answer the door. These are dangerous men, Harley. They want *me* but they'll take anyone if it means getting to me. Can you please stay with Abby for the night and hopefully the Chief will have some plan by morning. Thanks a lot Preacher Man, I owe you."

Harley heard the click of the receiver as he stood beside Abby in total darkness.

"I'm scared Harley. What if they come after us?"

"They know Howard is not here, so I think we're safe for now. There is a police car out front. Let's just be thankful we have no guests tonight. We'll go upstairs, near a phone and we'll take a few iron skillets with us, just in case." He gave her an exaggerated wink and smiled, as he pulled her along behind him.

CHAPTER 29

"Fear of man will prove to be a snare, but whoever trusts in the Lord is kept safe."

Proverbs 29:25

A strange-looking piece of moon scuttled behind the roof tops in New Hope as Howard and the Chief waited for word to come through the radios. The street lights cast an orange, shadowless glow, giving the town a drowsy ambiance, which also allowed oncoming lights to be seen in advance. A distant train whistle was the only sound amid the darkness.

Howard had been in many menacing situations in his lifetime when he should have been petrified, but he always remained calm. Now, he could feel his panic rising, even though he was with the police, under their protection. His violence-as-usual policy was no longer in force and he was scared to death. He had been used to walking on the knife-edge of danger and now he didn't even know if he could use a knife. In the past, he carried a twelve-inch steel blade inside his boot. The thought of that now made his foot ache. Reflecting on his past, he realized how he grew up with such a casual acceptance of violence. Now, he wanted nothing to do with conflict. He was discovering a whole new way of life, filled with harmony and he liked it. He wondered if someone had ripped out his heart and replaced it with a new one. Whatever the case, he was slowly coming to believe Miss Shirley's philosophy. Perhaps God did have him here for a purpose.

He tried to wrap his head around that concept but couldn't figure out how he would be able to help someone. All he ever did in his lifetime was hurt people. *Why would God pull him out of the filth and give him another chance? Nobody wanted him, not even his own mother, so why would God find him worthy?*

The chief was trying to get his attention by waving his arms. "Are you all right? The sun's almost up and we need to come up with a plan. I've already talked to Lilly, at the diner, and she's going to use her womanly wiles to get information out of King if he comes in for breakfast or lunch. All we can do is keep hoping he has a big appetite. We have no proof it was King last night who shot out the window and we don't want him to realize that we know he's in town. I'll order breakfast in, for both you and Freedom. Take the food and drive out to the farm. Explain to her what is happening and make sure she is safe. I wouldn't advise you to confiscate her gun but I do think you should ask her to put it away. We don't want any more hardship for that poor girl than she already experiences."

Howard was so glad for the plan the chief had come up with. Luring King out to the farm was brilliant. Wide out in the open meant less chance of innocent people getting hurt and there were plenty of hiding places for the police. It was also another opportunity for Howard to see the most remarkable woman he had ever met. There was just something about this girl named 'Freedom' that drew him into her world. Even though it was going to be a massive undertaking, he couldn't wait to help her totally restore her home and give her some kind of normalcy again. Deep down he wanted not only to help but protect her as well. He hoped that someday he could wear the kind of armor Miss Shirley had tried to explain to him, not only for protection for himself but for those surrounding him. The domain Freedom had created inside the farm boundaries was no longer enough. Her inquisitive, electric blue eyes had spoken far louder than her voice that day in the library and he needed to respond to that appeal.

Howard felt his recent visits to the farm had been productive. Freedom had allowed him to clear away overgrown bushes and remove dead trees shading the house, enabling the sun to generate more warmth inside her refuge. Her fresh homemade mint tea and honey-laden biscuits were now staples in Howard's daily routine. He worked as hard and as fast as he could, since time seemed to be important to Freedom. He sensed an urgency in her life and deemed it important to yield to her aspirations.

He had no idea what it felt like to fall in love with a woman, until now. He wanted to be with her every day. He had grown to love honey and creamed dandelion and he had learned how to use, what he called weeds, for healing. Freedom persevered in everything she did. Her strength and patience conquered more challenges than his hostility ever did. Just like him, she had endured the loss of parents, ridicule and bullying. But she reached to the depths of her soul, found her essence and stayed true, unlike himself, who had allowed King to intrude in his space and seize his spirit.

To the outsider, Freedom was quirky, but she had discovered herself early on, as she stood on solid ground. She had never allowed anyone to influence her, except her parents. Her mother was kind and submissive to her father until he began drinking. Friends and family soon discarded them like old shoes and they became recluses. When Freedom's mother died, her dad turned to alcohol. Freedom had no one to turn to, except herself. She developed what some might call stubbornness but Howard had come to see it as an expression of strength. Even with all the thugs he used to hang with, none ever had the potential courage to stand alone. They had all leaned hard on Kingsley Spencer.

Howard, on the other hand, was a bit reluctant to peel back the many layers of his life and reveal his past. In her enthusiasm to comfort Howard, she was unknowingly helping to renew his trust in humans. Except for his friends at Summer Rain he never spoke of his former years to anyone. The chains of confinement, that he now realized existed, were slowly and methodically coming undone. King made it very clear that silence was not only golden but essential to his job. His appetite for the fast lane drove him to continue his work for King, allowing money to be substituted for love.

Each day Howard spent with Freedom allowed him to see a little deeper into her soul. It also allowed her to observe another human being. She absorbed Howard's kindness and his eagerness to help her. She listened to his stories of inside casinos and cried when he described King's treatment of cheaters. She also cried when Howard told her his life story and how it ended with his mother's death. She secretly cried at night, thinking of Howard's dilemma with King. In her touch of rebelliousness, she planned an intricate demise for the casino lord and even felt a smile cross her lips as she played it out in her mind. She could not tell Howard, but it seemed so satisfying to her every time she pictured it happening.

Howard was Freedom's proof that hope existed. The memories that scorched her fragile soul at one time were fading, allowing amnesia to conquer her ill-fated childhood.

Normally shy and very reluctant to speak to anyone, Freedom found her conversations with Howard to be encouraging but also confusing. She found herself voluntarily casting her stories of despair and hopelessness to Howard and it caught her off-guard. Swapping stories helped to uncover some major trust issues in both of their lives. Freedom realized that her stories were resonating with the same substance as Howard's. Trust no one. She had trusted her parents but they had let her down. She knew they loved her, but in the end, their addictions robbed them of their ability to share their love, even with their daughter.

Freedom appreciated Howard's concern as he offered her comfort and support, treating her like he had found her glass slipper. She revealed feelings to him she never knew existed, therefore validating a whole new way of life for her. Her theories about society sometimes became clouded when interacting with Howard. Even though he was surrounded with scoundrels for so many years, he somehow managed to protect a small part of his heart from those who exploited him. He tried to convince her that humanity wasn't as bad as she believed. He expressed to her the kindness and compassion he had found when he came to New Hope. He told her about how he came as a mysterious stranger to Summer Rain and was embraced with kindness and compassion in his mission to find his brother.

Now he was on a different path, away from money and drugs, and for the first time ever, he understood the word 'peaceful.' He was getting used to a life filled with goodwill instead of malice. He was denied this liberality for the first twenty-eight years of his life, but from here on out, he wanted it to be different. He needed to be emotionally and physically free of King before he would be able to consciously unravel his crumpled emotions and salvage what remained. He hoped he and Freedom could untangle them together. Howard was exceeding the speed limit but he needed to get to Freedom's and prepare for King's visit. Freedom appeared at the front door and smiled when she caught his eye. "You seem to be in quite the rush this morning. You have a lot of work to do today?"

"Sit down, Freedom. There is something I need to tell you and I have to say it quick."

Freedom could see the battle going on inside him as she chewed worriedly on her bottom lip, but she said nothing.

"Remember when I told you about working for a man named King? Well, he's in town and he's looking for me. He knows I'm here and I think he's on his way. I want you to stay hidden and let me handle this. The police are going to be close by in case I need them."

This time, Freedom interrupted before he could continue. "I will not stay hidden. This is my farm and if any kind of battle is going to happen, I'm going to be on the front line. You are the one who should hide. Let me handle this joker. My old rifle will make him dance."

"Trust me Freedom, his will make you dance just as fast and he would have no problem aiming at your heart."

"I'm not leaving here so I need you to trust me. If you want the police to catch him in a premeditated plot, then you leave it to me. Remember all the trips I make to the library? What kind of books do you think I read?"

"I don't know, I never really thought about it."

Eyes shining with mischief and excitement she said, "I read mysteries – with lots of gunfights and murders."

Howard looked at her and laughed. "Reading about something and actually doing it are quite different. King is dangerous and he doesn't care who he hurts. He's been doing this for so long he's convinced he will never get caught, especially in such a small town."

"Please trust me, Howard. I can handle this and it's my payback for all you are doing for me."

A loud knock on the door sent both of them scrambling into the bedroom. As Freedom gently pushed him into a closet, her eyes demanded that he stay. She gestured for him to be quiet by putting her finger to her lips and before he had a chance to move, Freedom disappeared.

CHAPTER 30

The words of his mouth are wicked and deceitful
he has ceased to act wisely and do good

Psalm 36:3

Gripping the steering wheel more tightly than usual, King ignored the voice of caution. He was going about this all wrong. Shooting out a window in the police station was not real intelligent. Knowing what he just did sent pure rage through him. Violent images lurched obscenely inside his skull causing him to seethe with anger and humiliation. *I am Kingsley Spenser and my reputation precedes me. When I implement a plan, it isn't supposed to fail. The strategy is to find Howard and bring him back or assassinate him in the process. Why did I let my disappointment with Howard break my number one rule - never get angry.* Getting even leaves a better impression. Anger causes exposure to weakness and weakness leads to failure.

King scolded himself again, this time talking out loud with a few curse words thrown in. Sitting here in the dark was not going to resolve the problem. He drove towards the airport, planning to exchange the rental car for a different make and model. He would then go back to the hotel and devise a new plan. Morning was only a few hours away and he would revisit the diner, this time sitting in the corner, hiding behind the newspaper. There was no way anyone in this town, with the exception of Howard, would be able to identify him. No one even knew he was here. A lot of time passed since the betrayal and his hope was that Howard would assume he was free of his obligations and recklessly familiarize himself with a whole new life. King smiled as he thought about Howard being so foolish. He was sure he taught him better than that.

He exchanged the car for a gray mini-van and felt sure he would blend in well with small town traffic. He returned to the diner and found the same pretty waitress pouring coffee to customers. He slid into the corner booth and motioned for Lilly to bring him a cup of coffee. She grabbed a menu from the stack and laid it on the table next to his cup.

Feeling a little nauseated, Lilly pasted on a smile as she spoke. "Hi. I see you decided to stay a few more days. I thought you were just passing through but I'm glad you came back for more of our food. Would you like another omelet today or would you like our special, which is a ham and cheese sandwich?

King was flattered that such a fine-looking young woman would remember him and his food choice. Maybe he could take advantage of this flirtatious little honey. A satisfied light came into his eyes, "You remembered me and what I ordered?"

Lilly's eyes also exhibited a light, but it was more like a fire from an arsonist ready to strike a match. She wanted this guy to go up in flames. Pouring this man a new cup of coffee allowed her time to ask in her own sassy sweet way, "Who did you say you were in town to see?"

King's tone was a little chilly. "I don't believe I dropped a name."

Lilly, still pretending she was part of James Bond's entourage, moved closer to King, causing her few nose hairs to wilt under the strong, citrus scent of his after-shave. "I'm sorry, I was sure it was you who told me you were looking for some guy by the name of Howard." Lilly wrinkled up her face and smiled, "I do have a lot of customers coming in here every day and sometimes they tell me all about their troubles. I guess it must have been someone else. I'm really sorry."

"No, that's okay, I guess it would be hard to keep everyone's conversation separate. But I'm not really looking for anyone. I told you, I'm just passing through."

Lilly's smile faded a little as she kept talking, as though King's remark hadn't even been heard. "That's kind of an old-fashioned name isn't it? Who would name their kid that?" She pulled some creamers from her pocket as she continued. "Are you sure you're not looking for a Harold? We have quite a few guys with that name. In fact, our best man's name was Harold, except everyone calls him Hoafie. If you called him Howard, he would probably answer you cause he's not the brightest of lightbulbs. I love him to death but it is what it is." She shrugged and casually got a little closer to the table, "I just remembered - there was a man in here last week who was trying to hit on me and he said his name was Howard." Lilly laughed and remarked how odd that was. "He seemed like a real nice fellow. Said he was new in town."

Now not only did King's eyes light up but so did his whole-body demeanor. He was trying to act nonchalantly but Lilly could see the wheels turning inside his head.

"I think you have me confused with someone else. I told you I'm not here to meet anyone." A wicked, feral smile curved King's lips as he persisted with the conversation. "You didn't tell your husband about this guy, did you? He might be a bit jealous."

"Oh, yes, I did and he was ready to march right out to that old dilapidated farm and kick his butt."

"What old farm would that be? Everything I've seen around here looks pretty well kept."

"Oh, there's an old farm out on Route 6. It's well hidden from the road. I've heard this guy is trying to buy it so he goes out there and just sits alone, like he's daydreaming or something." She straightened his napkin and said, "Aren't people really weird?"

"Yes, yes, they are. I have to go." He swung his legs out from under the booth but Lilly blocked his way.

"Please excuse me. I really need to go."

"But if you leave without ordering, I'll get in trouble. My boss will dock my pay. He'll blame me for saying something that made you leave. We call him Hawkeye cause he watches us every second. Please, I need this job."

Lilly could see the anticipation of finding Howard coming out every pore in King's body.

He was barely able to sit still, making Lilly smile as she continued her award-winning performance. King slid back into the booth and asked how long it would take if he ordered an omelet.

"Are you in a hurry? I thought you were just relaxing in our little town."

"I am, but I want to do some sightseeing today so I'd like to get an early start."

"Eggs and toast coming right up!"

Lilly hurried to the kitchen and called the Chief. "He took the bait. Hook, line and sinker."

"Good work, Lilly, we'll take it from here."

She returned to King's table and apologized for the delay of his food.

Another satanic smile spread across King's lips as he took a long drink from his cup. It was going to be a good day. *I can just make Howard disappear and no one will miss him.* He smiled, thinking Christmas had come early.

CHAPTER 31

Guard me, O Lord, from the hands of the wicked;
preserve me from violent men, who have planned
to trip up my feet.

Psalm 140:4

Freedom picked up her gun on the way out the back door. She hoped her demands on Howard were enough to keep him hidden. She smiled as she played over in her mind the plan she had for the monster at her front door.

By the time she reached the front yard, King was already walking down the path toward the barn. He sure was making this easy for her.

King was focusing on his surroundings, thinking it was like standing in the middle of a time capsule. The old cement-block silo stood in the shadow of the faded red barn and the huge oak trees that mushroomed above the roof top. Grape vines were trying to survive on fences where blue ripened grapes supplied bees with nectar for their honey. A broken-down tractor still hitched to the plow, waiting for its driver, looked lonely as it sat near the barnyard. There were a few cows mingling inside the fence but otherwise, all was quiet.

Freedom watched as he inspected Howard's car, opening the passenger side door and foraging through the glove box. Finding nothing of interest there, he walked around to the driver's side and opened the door. Acting bored, he continued towards the barn. Freedom changed direction and proceeded toward the cow stalls in the lower level of the barn. There she waited with rifle in hand. She had never fired the gun but she knew she could. She waited as King kept getting closer until he was close enough for her to smell some god-awful stink. She smiled as she checked out his fancy car and expensive clothing, yet he smelled like he had come in contact with a ripe old polecat. She didn't need some swanky perfume, especially if it smelled like this man. Roses from her garden was her fragrance of choice.

"Ya know mister, you ain't the first critter I've caught sneakin' around my farm but you just might be the last."

King almost swallowed his tongue. He felt the cold metal on his neck as she spoke.

"I'm sorry ma'am, but I'm not sneaking around. I'm just looking for the owner. I tried knocking but nobody came to the door."

"Well, most people I reckon would just leave and come back another time instead of pokin around other people's property. Who are you and what do you want?"

"My name is Tom Smith. I buy and sell property and I hear this farm might be for sale. I just came out to take a look around."

"Well, it ain't for sale so you can just move your fancy behind back to your car and move on out of here." Freedom moved the barrel of the gun lower to the middle of his back but as she did, he turned and, with one quick swipe of a knife he slashed her arm, causing her to drop the gun. Her reaction was swift as she spun and placed a front snap-kick to King's groin. The pain streaked up to his stomach and an animal instinct told him all was not well. He drew his hand back and struck out, but Freedom leaped to the side. As he reached in his boot for his .44 Bulldog revolver, he felt another boot being slammed into his stomach, choking off his breath. He fell to the ground as he heard the unmistakable cluck of a hammer being cocked.

When King looked up, his eyes widened in alarm. A familiar pair of cold eyes darkened dangerously as they stared at him over the gun barrel.

"Howard, you're alive! I'm so glad to see you. You can put that gun down. I'm here to take you back home with me. I've been looking for you for a while now. Why didn't you call me?"

"Really? You're asking me why I didn't call you? I think you're smart enough to figure that out. I'm never going back with you. You need to go and leave me alone."

"Son, what are you talking about?"

"I am not your son so don't call me that."

Howard was still pointing the gun at King, determined to force him from the property and out of his life, when Freedom's scream chilled him to the marrow. Howard saw a wink of metal flashing in King's palm and seconds later he felt the sharp jabbing pain, like an icicle lodged in his stomach. King was fast and Howard should have been prepared for one more gun hidden in the master's boot. Howard panicked as a pool of blood flowed from the gaping hole in his gut. The last thing he remembered was seeing King pointing the gun at Freedom.

King could feel his power rise in this silent battle of wills. No one would find these two in this remote part of the country and soon Howard would bleed to death. His little lover would follow. King continued to hold the gun at chest level, ready to fire when Freedom's jeans, so snugly molded to her hips and thighs, caught his attention. The nubile curves beneath her faded t-shirt seemed to be calling his name. She had quite the seductive young body and he was not the kind of man to deny himself carnal pleasures. They were alone, except for Howard, and he was out cold. He always wanted to have a good roll in the hay and, as he laughed out loud, he appreciated the fact that he could now make that cliché authentic.

Freedom watched his eyes grow hungry as he shouted, "Young lady, let's you and I take a short walk." He pointed the gun in the direction of the barn and said, "Move!"

Freedom walked as slowly as she could, hoping Howard would wake up and rescue her. She turned around for a glimpse but he was still lying on the ground. *I can't let this guy take me to the barn. There has to be a way to escape.* They were inside the barnyard stepping around cow piles when King stepped *into* a pile causing him to slip and fall, launching the small pistol into the air. It landed in the middle of a huge mound. King's vanity kept him from plucking the weapon from the poop, but he remained in control by whipping out a lethal-looking switchblade. Freedom dove for the airborne gun but missed. She had to reach the dung before King could slash her again. She figured this was as serious as catching on fire so she tucked and rolled, just like she had seen in a book. King lunged at

Freedom but underestimated her actions and once again landed in a pile. Freedom reached for the gun and aimed. The bullet ricocheted off a rock and struck King in the leg. More curse words than Freedom ever heard came spilling out of his mouth while he tried to run toward her. She fired again. This time she knew the bullet had struck a more vital part of his body. He fell back from the impact and was screaming like a stuck pig. Ignoring him, knowing he was now powerless, she ran to Howard. He opened his eyes as she lifted his head onto her lap.

"Help me to my car and get me to the hospital. Can you drive a car, Freedom?"

"No, but I'll just call that 911 number. They'll come for you."

Howard's eyes impaled her. "You have a phone?"

"Not exactly, but I do have a CB. Just as good as a phone." She unbuttoned his shirt and applied pressure to the wound with her sweater. "Don't move Howard, I'll be right back." She laid his head down gently and ran to the house.

Within minutes two squad cars screeched into the driveway, sirens blaring. Chief McDonald leaped out of one of them. "An ambulance is on the way, Howard."

"About time, glad you could make it," Howard said with mock sarcasm.

While the EMT's laid Howard on the gurney, the Chief fired back, "When you're in better emotional and physical condition, I'll explain my tardiness."

King pointed at the ambulance and at Freedom. "They tried to kill me! You need to arrest them. Why don't you have handcuffs on them?"

"Officer Smith, this fellow wants to know where our handcuffs are! Could you oblige him and show him how they work?"

"Be happy to, sir."

"You're arresting me? What about those two? They attacked me and I defended myself. I want a lawyer."

The chief gave a disgusted wave with his hands as he explained, "Oh you'll have time for that. Right now, I guess we better get you to the hospital. Throw him in the back seat, boys, and make sure you hit every pot hole on the way."

King laughed bitterly as pain swept through him. "You boys will pay for this. I'll be out before the sun comes up and I suggest you all buy mirrors so you can watch your back."

Chief McDonald leaned in through the back window and informed King about the amount of charges they had against him. Enough to put him in jail for the rest of his life. "Your casino days, or should I say nights, are over."

King's muscles tightened, his head drew back stiffly.

"What's the matter, pal? Did you really think we didn't know you were in town? We've been watching you for days. Pretty good for small-town cops, huh?"

A loose thatch of hair fell across King's forehead as he glared mindlessly out the window. A look of disbelief, rage and frustration distorted his face; he had the withered look of an empty balloon.

Freedom smiled as she watched them drive away with King. She read about things like this happening, but to have it happen in her own yard was scary. She was concerned about Howard but did not want to ride in the ambulance. Suspecting some sort of anxiety, the chief talked softly to Freedom and asked if he could drive her out to Summer Rain. Abby and Harley would know how to guide this brave young woman.

Abby and Harley were so pleased to know the chief had that much confidence in them. They welcomed Freedom with open arms and tried to make her as comfortable as possible. A hot shower washed away the mud and manure but it couldn't wash away her anxiety. More than the water washing over her, was the realization that she'd allowed herself to be separated from her home. What would happen to her now? She had learned to live in an isolated world. Would she be able to adjust to having people around? She had never been in anyone else's house before and, even though she knew this was safe ground, she could not stop herself from wanting to go home.

She found her way to the kitchen, where Abby and Harley were waiting, and said, "I would like to visit Howard but I've never been in such a big building with so many people."

Hearing the panic in her voice, Abby eased her concern by saying, "We understand, Freedom. We have a call in to the hospital and they have promised to call us as soon as Howard is out of surgery. We will take you to see him, but if you don't feel comfortable making the trip, Harley will go visit Howard and you and I will stay here. Chief McDonald would rather if you do not go home yet, just in case someone comes looking for King."

Abby saw Freedom was about to protest. She smoothed her brow with the intimate touch of a mother, and interrupted, "It's okay dear, you can stay here for as long as you need. Harley will take you home every day to take care of your animals, and the Chief is keeping a police car on duty for the next couple of weeks. We would just feel better if you stayed here with us."

CHAPTER 32

*For the wrongdoer will be paid back for the wrong
he has done, and there is no partiality.*

Colossians 3:25

The next few weeks proved to be quiet at Summer Rain. King was sentenced to 35 years in prison with no chance of parole. Howard was forced to testify against the casino tycoon and because he did, was granted a plea-bargain by the courts. He agreed to give evidence against King in exchange for amnesty for the deceit he had executed on hundreds of gamblers. The judge determined that, given his age and no parental guidance, Howard had been coerced into the life of a swindler by Kingsley Spencer. The judge thought his appearance in New Hope to find his brother was a subconscious means of escape from a life of crime. He commended Howard on his honorable decision.

Howard spent one week in the hospital and was discharged with a clean bill of health. The bullet entered through the front of his stomach, barely missing his intestines, nicking his colon and making a clean exit through his back. Surgery repaired the colon and daily dressing on the exit wound allowed him to walk in two days.

Harley drove Howard to Summer Rain and surprised him with the presence of Freedom. The world seemed to shift beneath his feet when she fell against him, taking him by surprise.

"Howard, I'm so glad you're okay. I'm sorry I didn't come to the hospital but I knew you would understand."

He reached up, unhooked her arms from around his neck and whispered, "I'm so glad you're here and safe. I'm the one who should be sorry. I never meant to put you in the middle of danger."

Freedom shuddered, protecting that place in her heart only Howard had reached. She felt vulnerable to the unexpected affection he was showing her, yet she longed for more.

Freedom's voice was fragile and shaky as she answered. "Please do not be sorry. I am so happy too that you survived a gunshot. I never would have thought it possible."

She looked at Abby and spoke freely about what she was thinking. "I don't know how to express my gratitude to you for allowing me to stay here this past week. You have been so kind and I have learned so much. But if it's okay I would like to go home. I'm excited to try some of the recipes you shared with me." Her smile broadened as she bit back a soft appreciative moan. "I've never had such good food."

If Howard hadn't already convinced himself that he was in love with this woman, he knew it was true now. She was so pure, so innocent of all the world's problems. Someone from the outside looking in on her lifestyle would accuse her of being very peculiar but her little corner of the world was exactly where she wanted to be and now it was where Howard wanted to be, too. He thought again about Miss Shirley and her influence on him. She brought him across the bridge further in a few months than all the people combined in his lifetime. It just went to show how important it is to have positive people around during your childhood. His only regret in life was not knowing Miss Shirley earlier. He might have saved himself and a lot of other people a great deal of unnecessary heartache.

"Howard would you be able to take me home? I have some things that need tendin' to."

"I'll go get the car right now."

Freedom gave Abby one last hug before going out the door and promised to come visit with Howard. As Abby watched her two new friends drive down the driveway, tears rolled down her cheeks. They were tears of sadness for Shirley's absence mingled with tears of joy for Howard and Freedom's future. Abby wanted to have a positive impact on Freedom's life as much as Shirley had hers.

CHAPTER 33

Many are the plans in the mind of a man,
but it is the purpose of the Lord that will stand.

Proverbs 19:21

Freedom leaned against the open kitchen window allowing the breeze to blow her hair. The air current brought the promise of spring into the room as it vibrated with the sound of the robin's song. The day began peacefully before her as she noticed the tiny crocus blooms that fought their way from underneath the wounded clumps of grass in her yard, creating a patchwork of purple and yellow.

Despite the farm's reputation, it was no longer the dilapidated, ready-to-fall-down property that caused everyone's imagination to work overtime throughout the years. Howard worked miracles with the property. No more overgrown bushes or falling limbs from trees. All the fences were mended, keeping her few animals enclosed and out of her garden. He restored the barn back to its original color with a new coat of paint.

Freedom watched Howard pull into the driveway, get out of the car, rest his hip on the front fender and cross his arms over his chest. What exactly was he doing?

He seemed to be in deep thought, as if the weight of the world were on his shoulders. She would be concerned if it weren't for the contentment in his eyes, as he stared at the barn and its surroundings. He reminded Freedom of an artist taking time to appreciate his work. She wondered if his broad shoulders ever tired of the burden he still carried. She knew he had many regrets about his time with Kingsley Spencer, and if he were truthful, she was sure he still felt pain when he thought of his mother.

Freedom remained by the window enjoying the scenery, realizing that Howard had become the center of her attention. If not for him, she would still be alone, living behind closed doors. His stubborn pursuit had undeniably altered her judgment of everyone beyond the fences of her farm. She would forever be grateful. He gave her hope to think that change is possible, even when you're living in the middle of a raging storm. He revealed his character with his honesty and considerate ways. He attested to the importance of choices, convincing her to believe in herself and to choose the remedies from her heart, not her head.

She knew he regretted so many of the choices he made in the past, but he had also admitted that without those lessons he would not be able to recognize the difference between morality and immorality. He had told her about Miss Shirley's belief that God had put him on earth for a purpose and by living on both sides of the track, he would find his way.

Howard walked toward the barn, needing a different view of his newly-found habitat. As he situated himself on the fence, he caught a glimpse of Freedom peeking out from behind the curtain in the kitchen. Even though he knew she understood his need to be alone at times, he stared past her beautiful face into his own thoughts and pretended not to notice her.

There really hadn't been much time for Howard to think about the search for his brother, with all the work at the farm and cooking at the Inn. He fell into bed at night, exhausted. As time passed and food preparation became more routine at the Inn he also became more accustomed to the demanding work of a handyman. Freedom helped him by working out a schedule for each day. He taught her his culinary skills and was pleased to find that she was an excellent student. She was still not comfortable with serving the guests, but with encouragement from Abby, her insecurities seemed to be weakening.

Life was good for Howard and he was loving every minute of it. He finally understood the fundamental appreciation for life. Living simply and allowing the earth to provide for you was definitely an unfamiliar practice for him. He had never seen the inside of a barn or a bale of hay until he met Freedom. He smiled as he thought about her name. He had wanted freedom for so long and now he had it, both physically and psychologically. Sometimes he was spell-bound with thoughts that were new and compelling, like honesty and responsibility. His child-like craving for a father figure had drawn him into the world of deception and ruthlessness. King had charmed him with gifts and insincere respect, making him believe he was only worth something in the world of casinos. In the past, Howard had no conception of how isolated King had made his life but living in the country had emancipated him. He was now free of guilt and regret.

Freedom, the woman he was in love with, and freedom, the liberation from evil, caused his body to vibrate with new life. He was now sure of himself, his thoughts clear and unfettered, anticipating true contentment with his new-found family.

Freedom was arranging a new bouquet of roses when she felt a hand descend on her shoulder from behind. She turned quickly and came face to face with Howard as she declared, "I guess you think you're pretty sneaky huh?"

"Not sneaky, just lonely."

"You seemed to be in deep thought out there on the fence. Something I should know about?"

"I think you already know all my thoughts, especially since they are usually about you."

He stood so close she could feel the heat from his body, the whisper of his breath on her cheek. Even though a low moan slipped past her lips, a husky helpless sound of want, she felt uneasy at the sudden physical intimacy. Somewhere between suspicion and enchantment she felt herself flowing toward him, her common-sense skittering into the shadows.

Surrendering to the crush of feelings that drew them together, Howard's head lowered and his mouth moved over hers with exquisite tenderness, a light teasing kiss, just enough to still her resistance. He laid his cheek against the crown of her head and inhaled the fresh scent of roses. Gripped with sensations that were new and inevitable, caused Freedom to tremble in his arms. Sensing this, Howard began courting her senses with gentle persuasiveness, allowing her to relax. As soon as she leaned into his embrace, this newly-awakened response to life began to comfort her.

"Freedom, I want you to know that just now, when I kissed you and held you, it felt like I came home. This is where I want to be. Right here on the farm with you. I realize I don't need the wild life anymore." There was a calmness in his eyes as he continued, "I never before lived in a peaceful environment and every time I step foot inside your gate, there seems to be a sense of peacefulness that comes over me and for the first time in my life, I find myself actually *looking* at a blade of grass instead of just walking on it. I see things now that I never saw before. It's as if you poured buckets of paint on everything and brought new color to the world. I know that may sound corny but it's true." He lifted one brow in admiration as he tried to remember, "Isn't there a song that says I was blind but now I see?"

Freedom smiled and softly said, "Yes, and it's called Amazing Grace."

"I never understood what that line meant but meeting you has opened my eyes from the blindness that I've been living with. Impaired vision I didn't even know I had." He flashed a captivating smile as he continued, "How ironic that it was your eyes I first saw in the library that changed my ability to see things differently. They left me spell bound. I had to find out whose eyes they were."

Freedom was so immersed in Howard's words, she never heard the teakettle whistling. Howard leaned back, turned off the stove and waited for a response from the woman he knew was truly his soulmate. At the moment though, her incredible eyes were narrowed in concentration, but still not convinced the words she was hearing were meant for her. He went to the stove and poured the boiling water into her favorite tea cup. He watched as the honey slowly disappeared from the dipper into the hot liquid. It was a small gesture but he knew it delivered a message that only she would understand. He served the tea with a napkin, a spoon and two cookies, just as she had taught him.

Her smile broadened in approval as she realized his words and actions had deeper significance today. She felt his strength as it surrounded her, creating more determination in his quest to convince her that he was no longer a man of the past, but a man with a future.

A little ball of need burst in the pit of her stomach, melting her resolve, intensifying her feelings for this man who had scooped in and rescued her from a quarantine life. She could feel the struggle going on inside Howard's heart as he tried to stifle his impatience with this one-sided conversation. His cologne, a rich dark fragrance, drifted by her nostrils provoking her brain to return to reality.

"I'm sorry Howard. I got a little lost with what you just said to me. Those are all new words and I have to focus." Her fingers drummed distractedly on her crossed knee as she spoke, "I appreciate and feel honored that you consider me so important in your life. I think I feel the same way about you, but since I have nothing to compare you to, I'm a bit anxious about a relationship. I'm willing to continue getting to know each other and if you would like, you may stay in one of the spare bedrooms. I know business has picked up at the Inn, so if you move here, it will free up another room for Abby to rent. You can give her car back, too, if you are able to get the old truck, that's out in the barn, to run again." She was almost embarrassed at how happy it made her to think that he would be residing at the farm.

"Really, Freedom? You would let me do that? I promise I'll be a total gentleman until you're ready for the next step in this relationship."

"I've been alone a long time and, as much as I no longer want that, I'm also scared."

"I know you are, and as much as I have always been surrounded by people, I've also been alone my whole life. I keep repeating Miss Shirley's philosophy but every day I'm more convinced that she was right. God does have a purpose for everyone on this planet and I think you and I are going to find out together exactly what that might be.

Chapter 34

Nothing is covered up that will not be revealed,
or hidden that will not be known.

Luke 12:2

Howard moved his meager belongings into the room with the window facing the barn. This way he could see any activity with the animals or unwanted guests. He and Freedom had settled into a routine that seemed to satisfy each of them.

"Good morning Howard. Did you sleep well?"

"Yes, thank you, how about you?"

"Fine. I've already taken care of the animals so you are free to go to the Inn a little early today, unless you have something else you want to do around here."

"As a matter of fact, there is something I want to talk to you about. It was put on the back burner for a while now and I think I need to start searching again."

"You mean your brother?"

"Yes, I have finished most of the major projects here on the farm and the Inn is running quite smoothly so I need to take some time to look for my brother. Are you interested in helping me?"

Freedom never felt so fully alive. Excitement raced through her as she ran to get her shoes and jacket. "Where are we going to look first?"

"Slow down, woman, we need a plan." He ran a hand through his thick hair and sighed. "Sit down here so we can talk about this."

Freedom grabbed a notebook and planted herself at the kitchen table. "Let's write down everything you know, just like the detectives do it. You talk and I'll write."

"You're really excited about this aren't you?"

"Do you realize how lucky you will be if you find your brother? I always thought it would be great to have a brother or sister, so yeah, I'm excited for you to find him." She leaned toward him eagerly and asked, "What do you know so far?"

"All I really know is that I have a brother. I'm assuming he is older than I, but I don't know for sure. Howard heard the anger in his own voice and forced himself to project a calmer tone. "My mother didn't have any more time to explain before she passed away."

Freedom, hearing the despair in his voice, decided today might not be the day to talk about finding his brother. She decided to distract him somehow so she began talking about the two cows that had died this year. "I'm going to be a little short on cash because of their deaths. The local butcher had already agreed to buy them but now, of course, he can't. My vegetables haven't done very well this year either, so I won't have much income. I think there might be some items in the attic that I could take to the flea market and sell but I'm a little leery of going up there by myself. My parents were like packrats and I know the space is bursting at the seams. Do you think we could go up there today and look around?"

Grateful for the diversion, Howard agreed. "Grab your tea and let's go."

As Howard opened the door to the attic he was struck by the thought he had never even seen an attic. He grew up in apartments where attics didn't exist. His nostrils were attacked with the scent of dust along with the stink of mildew as it hung heavily in the stale air. There was a faint scent of marijuana in the drug paraphernalia still spread out on top of an old battered bench. Rodents had used any left-behind grasses for nesting, leaving proof of their existence everywhere.

He looked at Freedom, hoping she would be turning to leave, but instead she had tears running down her cheeks. "I know this is bad, Freedom, it's making my stomach do somersaults, too, but you don't have to do this. I'll find some guys in town to help out."

"It's not that, Howard. Everywhere I look here, I see my parents. I knew they did drugs but I was too young to really understand, and now that I do, I find it incredibly sad."

"I'm in total agreement with you but if I've learned anything over these past few months it's that there is always hope. Just being around positive people like Harley and Abby and of course, Miss Shirley, taught me it's never too late to change. A year ago I was an angry, immoral young man with a chip on my shoulder the size of Texas and ready to fight everything and everybody." He reached for her hand, tucked it comfortably between his and let out a short laugh as he said, "Now look at me. I'm the epitome of angelic!"

His teasing broke the tension of the moment and she, too, allowed her gentle laugh to ripple through the air.

"I just don't want to waste my life like my parents. They were good people but they had no guidance, no one who cared. They got lost in the confines of this farm and their remedies for life. I have had anxiety about that all my life but until you came along I, too, was lost in thinking that no one cared."

"That part of life is over for both of us. We do have people now that care about us and we have hope for the future. We have Abby to help with our social skills and Harley for our spiritual guidance. Even if I never find my brother, my life will be complete just having you as a part of it."

"Thank you, Howard, but I want to help find your brother. First, let's start cleaning up this mess. Maybe we'll find something of value that will bring us some income. Who knows what kind of treasure is waiting for us under the eaves."

Howard lost track of how many times he went up and down the steep attic steps, carrying box after box of yellowed newspapers, magazines and books. Freedom wanted to sort through each box, hoping to find some memorabilia of her family. She was hoping to claim a legacy, a remnant of constructive evidence from her parents, giving her an entitlement to happiness. How ironic that she and Howard both seemed to be searching for the same thing--privilege and approval to grasp the true meaning of love.

"Exactly what are we looking for, Freedom? It's been three days and all I've seen are ads about food sales and local events. How many years' worth of newspapers are here?"

"I appreciate your patience and endurance but I just have this feeling that there is something in this attic that is important to me. You do not have to continue this. Take a break and go to the Inn. I'm sure they are waiting for you."

"You really wouldn't mind? I do have some things to get ready for dinner tonight." His lips brushed against hers as he spoke, "I'll be back to pick you up at seven."

As Freedom opened another box, something caught her eye. An old discolored candy tin with a red ribbon tied around the handles, holding it shut, was stuck in the back part of the carton. She easily tore the dry-rotted ribbon and opened the lid. It was filled with legal-looking documents attached to hand written letters. Curiosity won and she began unfolding each document. She found the deed to the farm, the title to the old truck, some documents specifying the authenticity of a few gold pieces, but nothing of any significance. The last document had been carefully folded and placed in a blue envelope with a logo stamped in the top left corner. The ink was worn but still visible enough to see the words, "The Cave."

Puzzled by the words, she turned over the envelope, only to see that it was still sealed. She debated whether to open it but it was addressed to her mother and legally she was next of kin. With trembling fingers, she broke the wax on the envelope and unfolded its contents.

It read, "Dear Effie, I know it's been a long time since we've had any contact but at one time you were my one and only friend. Do you remember when we used to hang out at the Double Dipper? Those were some great times. I don't know why we've allowed so much time to pass by without talking, but now it's too late.

Because of my continued drug abuse, I have been suffering with severe depression and paranoia. I have also been diagnosed with stage four liver cancer. Since I have no family, so to speak, I was hoping to make one last connection with you and tell you how much I appreciated our past friendship. You were the one person I could always count on.

I heard by way of the grapevine that you married that handsome John Hunter, had a daughter and moved to New Hope. I also heard you and John had occupied space at Woodstock and you were still pretty heavily into that scene.

I'm praying you're still together and happy. I got your address from Mrs. Crump. Remember how everyone called her 'Crump the Grump?' (I guess she wasn't as grumpy as we thought because she was real nice to me when I asked her for your address.)

Anyhow, here I am, waiting for an empty bed at the Holy Hill Medical facility (probably more like Holy Hell) wondering what will become of me, and wishing I had made better decisions in my life, such as holding on to my son. When he was three years old, his father, a wonderful man, died in a car accident. I never recovered from the tragedy and regrettably my son become a ward of the state. Since then, I have been in and out of hospitals but the treatments never seem to bring me the peace that I am seeking. After my husband's death, my way of life became perverted and saturated with drugs. I am told that because of my many years of abuse, I will probably be behind brick walls for the rest of my life. If you have any family Effie, take my advice and stay close to them. Being alone is a terrible cross to bear but looking back I can see that it has come about because of the stupid choices I made.

Life didn't treat me all that well but if I'd tried harder, I know I could have overcome all the obstacles. Hank had become my lifeline and when he died, I lost all hope. There was nowhere to go for support and no one except a three-year-old boy to love me and I failed him miserably. I don't know where you are in life Effie but keep trying. Don't give up on your husband or your children. It's all there is in life that really matters. I have many regrets but the one that eats away at me is my son. I have no idea where he is and no way to find out, so that is why I am entrusting you to help me. It's my last chance to do something right.

I am hoping you will find some way to find my son and give him his rightful inheritance, 'The Cave', and also my regrets about my absence from his life. If you cannot locate him within ten years from today's date, the property will become yours or one of your children's if you are no longer living.

I have kept my son's birth certificate and it is in a safe deposit box at the bank listed below. If you find someone who declares he is my son and you need proof, look on the bottom of his right big toe – there is a mark that resembles a cross. It is not very big so you will need to look closely. I'm not even sure if my son knows it's there. He was so young the last time I saw him, I didn't try to explain a birthmark.

Attached to this letter is the deed to the property on the south side of New Hope located at 4964 Trinity Street. It belonged to my husband and was known as 'The Cave' because of stories about the underground railway and slaves. It was a reputable bar that supposedly hid runaways in the back part of the building. It still operates as a bar but it is known under a different name, which I can't recall right now. The rent from this establishment has helped me get by when times were tough. The manager's name is 'Adam Draper.' The United National Bank handles all transactions and is aware of this contract. If you show this to them they will be obligated to allow you access to all accounts. I hope this will be an asset to you and your family and not a liability. I don't know your financial state, but please do what you need to do, even if that means selling it. My husband took great pride in the business established in this building and my wish is that it could be revitalized into something respectable for the community.

My lawyer, Grant Hayward drew up the paper work and I have attached it to this letter. May God bless you and yours as you remain on this earth.

Sincerely yours, Helen (Davis) Douglas

P.S. A key to the front door is taped inside this envelope.

Freedom couldn't believe what she just read. She never heard either of her parents talk about Helen. If only her mother had read the letter and taken her friend's advice, life might have been different for the Hunter family. Both parents might still be alive and relatively sober. She guessed she would always wonder why her mother never opened the envelope informing her of her newly acquired building.

As she sat with the paperwork in her hands, she imagined being a property owner of something besides a farm. She couldn't wait until Howard came home so she could share this information with him. He would know what to do.

On the way to the Inn, Freedom read the letter out loud to Howard, anxious for his response. When she read the part about the cave, he almost drove the car off the road. "Read that again Freedom. Did you say "The Cave?"

"That's what it used to be called. Why? Do you know where that is?"

Howard pulled over to the side of the road and leaned his head forward on the steering wheel. Could this be the cave he was looking for? Could he be one step closer to finding his brother? He was quiet for a minute, trying to absorb the possibility before he spoke. "This could be it, Freedom. This could be the place I find my brother! Let's show it to Harley and Abby, get their opinion and then tomorrow, as soon as it's daylight, you and I are going to "The Cave," he said, smiling ear to ear.

CHAPTER 35

And we know that for those who love God all things work together for good, for those who are called according to his purpose.

Romans 8:28

Freedom and Howard, neither one, got much sleep that night worrying about the validity of the document and what this meant for Freedom.

Early next morning she found Howard standing by the stove inhaling the wonderful aroma of bacon and eggs. She knew his little ritual always brought back memories of Shirley.

"Good morning, Sunshine. You look a bit tired. Something wrong?" he asked.

"No, I'm just anxious to see this building I've inherited. Can we leave right now?"

"Grab your coat, the address and off we go!"

The grime of the industrial revolution was still evident on many of the buildings in this part of town. As the first drops of rain dotted the pavement, Howard and Freedom ran down the sidewalk towards the huge brick building. The heavy front door had the look of a castle door with big black hinges and a small window for viewing. It was an old building but someone had obviously been maintaining it. A long corridor down the center separated the building. The right side was obviously set up as a bar, the left filled with husky oak tables covered in dust. A free-standing stairway of solid mahogany stood at the end of the hallway. Beyond that was a spacious solarium overlooking a long-forgotten garden. Neglected rose bushes tangled with mock orange vines crowded out all other plants and intruded upon the stone pathway. Freedom tried to imagine the beauty it must have once portrayed.

Howard was quite impressed with the overall condition of the building. It was old but he appreciated the amount of character. Even the dried-up wallpaper curled away from the yellow plaster, ready for something new. If only it could talk, he was sure it would have many stories to tell. Behind the bar, he found many unopened bottles of whiskey, rum, vodka and even some imported bottles of beer. Freedom was following him, silently. Howard wondered if someone had snatched her tongue.

Freedom's reaction was only silence. She couldn't seem to talk or even form facial expressions. Attempting to grasp the fact that it was all hers was putting her head in a full tailspin. Why had her mother never read the letter? How did it get in the candy tin? Did her father know about it? There were so many questions and no one to answer them.

Howard was watching Freedom and didn't want to interrupt her thoughts but she seemed overcome with emotion. "How are you handling all of this, Freedom? It's a bit overwhelming isn't it? I, myself, am a bit disappointed because I have seen nothing here to indicate that this building has anything to do with my brother."

She nodded her head in agreement as she climbed onto a bar stool and stared into the seemingly never-ending mirror behind the counter. This was totally outside her realm of thinking or doing. Did her mother purposefully ignore the contents of that letter or did it come at a time when marijuana had hold? There was no way to ever know the truth and if she were going to begin a new way of life, she would have to pull herself together. Howard was waiting for her to say something, but all she could do was smile a slow, trembling smile. She suddenly found herself being spun around and in one forward motion, she was in Howard's arms, burying her face against his throat.

Heat curled inside him, threatening his control, and just the scent of her hair presented a temptation that made him edgy. He pulled away from her and bowed politely, "Madam, you and I came here to solve a mystery and, as much as my heart wants to comfort you, logic is screaming, explore!

Where is that flashlight we brought along? We haven't seen everything yet."

Each room they searched appeared more ghostly than the last, with dusty, white sheets spread on top of meager furnishings. A sense of hollowness filled each space, eliminating the feel of hospitality.

Freedom opened the last remaining door and stepped inside a small apartment. She felt a slight breeze from the hallway, giving her the feeling that a message was being blown into the room. Each sheet covering the furniture was a different color, creating a rainbow effect. The pastels seemed to influence the entire mood of this room. She smiled, recognizing that this once was a happy place, unlike the other rooms. She walked through this modest apartment, discovering little toy race cars and baseballs. Obviously, a young boy had resided here, but why were his toys left behind? Freedom uncovered more items as she opened drawers. She envisioned someone crying as she walked out the door, leaving her life behind. Could it have been Helen? According to the letter, the death of her husband had ravaged her life, causing her to abandon hope. Even though Freedom had lost her parents at an early age, she would always remember them. But Helen's son, wherever he was, might have no memory of his mother at all.

Freedom's eyes had a burning, faraway look when Howard stuck his head inside the door. He wondered what she found in this room that would cause her to look so sullen. Remaining uncomfortably still, he waited. She turned to see him watching her, embarrassed at the tears that were running down her cheeks.

"What did you find, Freedom? Something about your mother?"

"I found toys, Howard, little boy's toys. Why would a mother make her son leave all his toys? The letter said her son was taken away from her but this looks like she just walked out and never looked back. It's just so sad."

"I know it's a heartbreaker but it's in the past and there's nothing you or I can do about it right now. I'm not making light of the situation but we need to concentrate on this building right now and figure out what we are going to do with it."

"I know, Howard, but there's something about this place that makes me want to stay. Do you not feel it? I don't believe in ghosts but I feel there is more than just you and me in this place. Walk with me into this tiny bedroom."

To humor her, Howard followed. A sudden sensation, a chill that crawled slowly over his body, generated memories before him, like a curtain just ripped aside. He saw visions of a man sitting on the edge of the bed reading to him, while his mother stood in the doorway, watching. As the image focused, he could also see trucks lined up on a shelf. The same shelf where his mother kept all his books. As another sharp memory sizzled through his brain, he heard the sound of his father's voice calling his mother. Helen – her name was Helen.

Arcing his arm through the air, Howard gestured at their surroundings as he turned to look at Freedom. He said the words cautiously, "This was my house. These were my things. I remember all of this."

Freedom stared at him. The lunacy of it was unsettling, yet intriguing, and she tried hard to comprehend what she was hearing. Silence filled the room as Freedom saw the struggle going on inside Howard. Then his smile said it all! His reaction was swift, as he swept her into his arms. "Do you know what this means, Freedom? I'm one step closer to finding my brother; at least I know I'm in the right town. Now, I know my mother really lived here. Wait 'til we tell Harley and Abby. They are going to be so excited."

"I don't think they can be any more excited than you are, Howard. You weren't even this thrilled when the police caught King."

"This is different. This is my real family." An eager look flashed in his eyes. "Do you realize I've never been able to say that before?" He began dancing around singing "I have a real family, I have a brother and I'm going to find him."

Freedom doubled over in laughter as Howard sang the same thing over and over.

Panting his way out the door, he grabbed Freedom's hand and sprinted down the steps to the bar. "I just had an epiphany! Do you know what an epiphany is, Freedom?' Not giving her time to answer, he picked her up again and swung her around. "It's the moment when a person understands and becomes conscious of something that is very important to him. Do you know what I just became aware of?" His eyes had cooled, sharpened and gone deadly serious. "Think Freedom, think!"

She had no idea what the correct answer should be, so she answered his question with one of her own, "What exactly are you talking about?"

"The name of this place used to be called 'the Cave' right?"

"Yes, but we've found nothing about your brother."

"But I *have* found evidence that *I* lived here so we need to keep looking. Let's bring Harley and Abby to help explore the place. There is something here, Freedom. I can feel it in my bones. I'm not giving up."

They both paused by the bar, silently wondering if the secrets it held would be revealed to them. Howard caught Freedom's hand and squeezed. His touch was reassuring and she was impressed with his obvious confidence.

CHAPTER 36

Who is the guarantee of our inheritance until we acquire possession of it, to the praise of his glory.

Ephesians 1:14

The front door opened and Harley asked Abby if she was expecting someone. Before she could answer, Freedom and Howard bolted through the kitchen, nearly exploding with anticipation of their news.

"Good morning. What's got you two in high gear?"

"You are never going to believe what we just found!"

Howard began talking about the building and the toys they found while Freedom launched into a description about some woman named Helen.

Harley approached the two with one hand held up like a traffic cop. "Both of you, slow down and give us the details, one at a time. Freedom, you first."

"No, Howard should be first, he has the most important news."

"But if it weren't for you, Freedom, I would have nothing."

Harley folded his arms over his chest and spoke loudly and firmly. "Howard, I designate you to tell your news first."

Tears were forming in his eyes even before he began to speak. "I am so close to finding my brother, Harley. I can feel it. Freedom brought a letter she found in her attic and it's about my mother. Once you read it, I think you will understand. She lived right here in New Hope and she willed a piece of property to Freedom's mom. That property, believe it or not, is where I lived! I found some of my toys. As soon as we walked in, I remembered my bedroom, the books and the little race cars that were left there. I know this is a major step to finding my brother."

Harley was speechless. He thought he should be reacting somehow to the information, but all he could do was stand in the middle of the room and watch Abby and Freedom as they hugged each other and cried. He was still reeling that he was now an engaged man. He wanted to tell the whole world, but he was hoping to have some time for him and Abby to process this next chapter in their life before jumping into the center of someone else's news flash. A ray of sun, shining through the windows, found Abby's ring and sent flickers of light through the room, but only Harley noticed. He smiled as he grasped the fact that the glory of his and Abby's big news would have to wait.

"Here's the letter and the documents, Harley, but you might want to sit down. This is pretty heavy stuff."

When Harley finished reading the packet he handed it back to Howard and said, "Are you sure about this, Howard? Sometimes we want something so bad we imagine things that aren't really there."

Howard cut a sharp look to Harley that dared him to argue as he began removing his sock. "I don't think I'm imaging this!' Sure enough, there under his right toe was a brown mark in the shape of a cross. Howard continued, his voice fragile and shaking. "I saw the toys, Harley, and I know they were mine. I remember that room."

"Okay, Howard, I believe you, but you have to admit, this all sounds a bit far-fetched don't you think?"

"I guess it does, but you keep trying to convince me that miracles still happen, so maybe this is one of them. Whatever it is, Freedom and I want you and Abby to go back to town with us and take a look. She's not sure what to do with it and I can tell she's a bit apprehensive about going to the bank. We need to hear all the details of this transaction, and she feels safe with you around. After all, who would try to hoodwink a preacher!"

Harley laughed, remembering Joan and how she had tried to fool him about her innocence concerning the embezzlement of church money. "It happens, Howard. Remind me some day to tell you about two years of my life. It's quite a story."

As they pulled up to the curb, Harley thought the building looked intimidating with its big castle-type door and bars on the windows. Its four stories seemed to loom over the empty lot next door creating ominous shadows on the rusty, abandoned cars. Howard opened the massive door and the four allies faced total darkness. Harley quickly switched on the lanterns, giving everyone's eyes time to adjust. Howard and Freedom began walking down the hallway but Abby and Harley stopped in front of the opening behind the bar and stared with wide eyes at an old wooden door kept shut with a hook and a protruding nail. "The Cave" had been scratched into the dense wood by a very steady hand.

Almost simultaneously, Harley and Abby called out for Howard to come see what they had found.

Howard hurried back, but when he saw their discovery he gave an impatient shrug. "Is that all you found? I saw that yesterday. It's just the name of the place."

Abby bristled a bit. "May I remind you, Howard, that we are here to help and we are going to push open the door. Now, if you don't want to see inside, then continue on your own search."

Harley, amused and surprised at Abby's response, smiled mischievously. "You better watch this one, Howard, she's on a mission and obviously has her own agenda."

Paying no attention to either man, Abby pushed opened the door, and was greeted with a strong smell of tobacco mingled with the scent of cheap scotch. She quickly covered her nose and waited for her eyes to adjust to the darkness. Harley held the lantern up towards the low ceiling and dangled it towards the shelves on the wall. "Stop Harley! Look! There are some names scratched onto that big stone. Bring the light closer so I can see." They all heard her sudden intake of breath.

"What is it Abby? What does it say?"

The shock caused the words to wedge in her throat and she struggled to find a way to speak. "Howard, I need you to tell me your middle name."

"Why?"

"Just tell me Howard. I need you to say out loud your birthdate, too." Anxiously he told her.

"Howard, this is the evidence you've been looking for! You're not going to believe it!"

"I need the lantern, Harley, I need to see for myself." When he held the light next to the names carved in the stone wall his eyes narrowed in concentration. "This is my name and birthdate."

By this time, Abby was crying and could only whisper, "Look over to the right, Howard. There is another name and birthdate. I think you've found your brother."

Howards hands trembled as he turned to see Harley staring at him curiously. It was at that moment that he saw the resemblance. He proceeded to give his brother a big bear hug, holding on tight.

"Okay, Howard what's this about? What did you see in there?"

"Look for yourself brother."

Harley grabbed the lantern and held it close to the carvings. There was his name, Harley Aaron (Davis) Davidson – November 10, 1956. He stood there in the hush, not knowing what to say or how to react. Silence consumed the small space as Harley waited for the others to speak. It seemed that no one knew exactly how to respond to the news.

Freedom was the first to give Howard and Harley each a hug, followed by Abby. Both women were still crying as Harley's vision wavered behind unshed tears. Howard, too, was having difficulty with blurred vision. The air was thick with emotions that no one seemed able to talk about right now. With arms around each other, they made their way outside to the car and returned to Summer Rain.

CHAPTER 37

Then the Lord God said, "It is not good that the man should be alone; I will make him a helper fit for him."

Genesis 2:18

The sun was rising to its height when Abby stood at the kitchen window, drinking her morning cup of tea. She watched as Harley bounded out of his car and practically ran up the front steps. She heard him open the door and within seconds, he was standing in front of her, staring at her with smoldering intensity.

"Are you okay, Harley? You flew in here like a winter snow storm. Is everything all right?"

"Couldn't be better, dear, but I need you to put down the tea and listen very carefully to me."

Abby could see the arteries throbbing in his neck, something that only happened when he was really nervous. What could he possibly be stressed about so early in the morning?

A calmness finally settled on Harley's spirit. He took her by the hand and led her out to the sunroom. "I know this is one of your favorite places, because you always think of Shirley when you're in here, but today I want you to concentrate on just us." He dropped down beside her on one knee and, without hesitation, pulled a velvet ring box out of his pocket and opened it up. "Will you ….. marry me?" Harley choked out the words.

Not responding, Abby stood in pleased surprise as her heart thumped hard and steadily against her chest. She had dreamed of this moment, but now that it was here, she felt her cheeks burning in memory of her first husband, Jeff. The nagging guilt that guarded her heart from another relationship was still there. She had no doubt she was in love with Harley and deep within, she knew Harley was in love with her, too. Even though she knew this day would come, she was not prepared for the grief blistering her heart with Jeff's memory. By opening the ring box, Harley had just opened the flood gates to her unforgettable past, causing memories to close around her and fill her with a longing to turn back the time. Harley was staring at her with a combination of confusion and disappointment. She could tell by the look on his face that he was feeling very unsure of his actions. Should she confess her guilty feelings to him or continue to hide them away?

Just as she was about to speak, Harley said shakily, "Abby, I guess I'm a bit stunned at your reaction. Not exactly what I was hoping for. Did I do something wrong?"

"No Harley, you've done nothing wrong. It's me that's acting foolish. I just had a flashback involving Jeff and I just didn't know what to do with it. I don't want any secrets between us, but I know this isn't the time to reminisce."

Harley's self-assurance took over as he stood and guided her to the sofa. He brought in a chair from the dining room, and with his knees touching hers, he began to talk. "When you have a deep wound, it eventually heals but almost always leaves a scar and sometimes that scar can hurt. If something happens that reopens the wound, of course you're going to feel pain." He shifted in his chair as he spoke, "I'm sorry I opened up that wound today but I had no idea the depth of your emotional scar." He lowered his head until their foreheads touched. "I chide myself for not knowing. As a pastor and your best friend, I should have been more conscious of your emotions concerning grief." He touched her hair, just a light stroke, and said, "You should not feel guilty. Jeff's death was an accident. You had no way to control that. The Bible says that God heals the brokenhearted and binds up their wounds. You need to let that happen." His fingers encircled hers, sending shivers up her arm. "I was so proud of the way you handled Shirley's passing. I watched you be ever so courageous, or so I thought. Why didn't you tell me how bad you were hurting?"

"I thought you would just know! I knew you were hurting too and I didn't want to add to anyone's sadness so I tried to act like Shirley. I thought it was working but for some reason I couldn't hold it in today."

Gently, Harley said, "There is a verse in Isaiah that says 'When you pass through the waters, I will be with you; and through the rivers, they shall not overwhelm you; when you walk through fire you shall not be burned, and the flame shall not consume you.' Obviously, you feel as if you've been flailing in the water and prancing over hot coals but take a look at yourself. You've committed yourself to helping those less fortunate than you and you're providing a place of rest for those who are weary. You have character, Abby. Character is mostly formed in the middle of a storm- a torrential downpour, such as you've experienced the last few years. Without knowing it, you were already equipped with an umbrella."

With tears streaming down her cheeks, Abby found it impossible not to return Harley's tender smile. "I love you, Harley Davidson, and the answer is yes, I will marry you."

"I have one more piece of scripture that I need you to hear and then I will not preach any more to you today. This is important, especially referring to the question I just asked you. 'And I will ask the Father, and he will give you another Helper to be with you, forever. John 14:16.' I hope you can believe that God has meant for you to be my helper."

Her heart reacted immediately to his words and she knew, without a doubt, his nearness would forever give her comfort.

CHAPTER 38

Whoever multiplies his wealth by interest and profit gathers it for him who is generous to the poor.

Proverbs 28:8

The next few weeks became a whirlwind at Summer Rain. Since Abby's acceptance of Harley's proposal, everyone was busy with wedding plans. The gazebo would once again host the joining of two people in love and the guest list would consist of family and a few friends. It was an exciting time for everyone involved.

Howard and Freedom knew they had found their soulmates and also knew marriage was in their future. The discovery of being a business owner brought a whole new dimension to Howard's perceptions and to his life. He could now appreciate the fact that even though it might not have been a good environment, God had allowed him to be a casino dealer, to prepare him for this next chapter in life. Memorizing numbers, working under pressure, and focusing, criteria that would all now work to his advantage.

Howard and Freedom were both attending a marriage counseling class and most importantly, they were becoming deeply involved in a Bible study group led by Harley. They were immersed in scripture and in awe of such new-found knowledge.

The shadow covering Freedom's farm was slowly disappearing as Howard continued to transform the shabby grounds into its once-charming homestead for Freedom.

The visit to the lawyer turned out to be bittersweet. Both Howard and Freedom were compliant with all the decrees listed but hearing the lawyer speak their mothers' names so often was a fresh reminder of the life the two women had sacrificed, even if by choice. They vowed with a new generation taking over, this time God would be involved.

With the deed to the building on Trinity Street also came a huge surprise from the bank. Helen had set up a trust fund for Howard, in the event he would be located, within 10 years following her death. The bank not only managed the money but was granted permission to wisely invest the income. Over 20 years had passed since the agreement was signed and fortunately, the bank made smart investments. It would take days for all funds to be calculated, but the lawyer estimated the total to be somewhere near $2,000,000 dollars. With genuine surprise on his face, Howard ran his hands through his hair in a detached motion, as in a dream.

The lawyer's words seemed to hang in the air as Howard gave a whistle of surprise. It was a new sensation to feel awkward, clumsy, even tongue-tied in any situation. He watched Freedom pinch her lower lip with her teeth, a habit he recognized as a sign of anxiety. He was surprised how nervous she was, so he made a mental note to reassure her that as long as she was with him, she would be safe. "Are you okay Freedom? You seem to be a bit uneasy."

"I'm fine. I just can't believe all of this is happening."

Putting his arm around her waist, he squeezed her affectionately. With his other hand, he turned the old-fashioned door knob that led them out of the lawyer's office. Once outside, the smell of approaching rain was heavy in the air. They reached the car in the nick of time and watched the rain streak the windows like tears.

They sat in silence for what seemed like hours and then, as if on cue, they both began talking at once. "What do you make of all this, Freedom? I can't believe I've been given a second chance like this, and such a wonderful chance at that." A smile slowly tipped up one corner of his mouth as he reassured her. "Just finding you was more than I could ever hope for. I've been thinking about how I am going to support you when we get married, since I have no tangible skills, but I guess my mother has taken care of that. I'm still trying to wrap my head around the fact that she saved all this money for me. She could have had a better life, yet she relinquished it so I could broaden my horizons, so to speak."

Freedom's eyes reflected her insecurity as she spoke softly. "I still can't believe your mother and mine were best friends. It's so ironic that they both, in one way or another, abandoned us and yet, here we are, together."

"I know, Freedom, but there is something I don't quite understand. How could your mother not know that my mother owned a bar in town? Why didn't they have physical contact? How did they get so far apart?"

"The only way I can answer is to explain that my parents were both recluses. My mother was usually stoned and possibly didn't even remember Helen. My dad would never have known your mother. The fact that we found her letter buried in the bottom of a tin box tells me that Dad never knew his wife had a best friend. New Hope is a fairly small town and one would think that Helen might have mentioned my mother's name to someone in the bar. On the other hand, the way I hear it, most townspeople found my family to be so disturbing. When Helen's husband died and she no longer operated the bar, who knows where she went. Obviously, she must have moved away and lost contact with my mother." She heard Howard sigh, weary of the conversation. "Let's get something to eat and continue talking about this later. I think Harley and Abby should hear all of this and advise us about these issues."

He replied with enthusiasm. "That's a great idea. I'm starving. I can whip up lunch at the Inn and then we'll talk to Abby and Harley.

CHAPTER 39

A friend loves at all times, and a brother is born for adversity.

Proverbs 17:17

Arriving home later than planned, put Howard into a cooking frenzy. There was only one couple staying at the Inn, but preparing dinner was still necessary. It was hard for him to concentrate on the strawberry sauce for the pork medallions, when all he could think of was the building on Trinity Street and what his mother must have gone through all those years ago. Abby's familiar voice tactfully lured him away from his past reflections and into the future. "What's for dinner tonight, Howard?" She popped a strawberry into her mouth while pulling up a bar stool. "I'm sure you're still staggering from this morning. What are you going to do with your building?"

"It's not my building. It's Freedom's."

"Harley said the document stated that it would rightfully be yours if you were found before the ten-year time period expired after the death of Freedom's mom."

Howard narrowed his eyes gauging whether she was telling the truth. "I guess I missed that part of the conversation this morning. Is what you just said, really true?"

"Howard, have I ever lied to you?"

No, but it's so hard for me to believe how this has all played out." He quirked his eyebrow questioningly. "You probably think God had a hand in all of this, right?"

"Can you explain it any other way?"

There seemed to be a flicker of interest in his eyes but Abby could tell he wasn't ready to throw in the towel just yet. He still displayed doubts about the power of God even though she could see his uncertainty weakening. The past year had brought many changes to this young man, most of which were probably unsettling to his heart and mind. Losing his mother and finding his brother were major milestones in his life. He wasn't used to trusting anyone with his personal thoughts, especially a woman or a pastor. Getting used to both did not happen overnight. She knew he was head-over-heels for Freedom and she was sure he was thrilled to find Harley, but adapting to this new way of life was somewhat intimidating. She sensed he really needed some one-on-one time with his brother.

Before Howard had a chance to respond to Abby's challenge, she slid another one of her opinions into the conversation. "After dinner tonight, I think you and your brother should sit down and have a chat."

As Abby's words sunk in, Howard couldn't help but savor his new-found enthusiasm for family. He never considered himself a weak man but he had never had a family before, either. Somehow, the thought of actually having a blood relative made him physically weak in the knees. He had always measured himself by skills mastered or missions accomplished and now all he needed to do was be himself. He really didn't know how to do that, but he was hoping Freedom and Harley would rally around him and show their patience.

Abby wasn't sure if Howard would take her advice so she made sure he was busy in the kitchen after dinner and alone with Harley.

Harley could hardly believe he was standing there watching his brother. The word had a nice ring to it but he was still trying to get used to the idea that he had a blood relative. He had never been told anything about his biological mother and now, after all these years, a brother appeared out of nowhere.

When Howard had showed up at the Inn, Harley had his suspicions, but as time went on he and Howard formed a friendship. He found it astonishing how God created each man from the same woman, made them so different and yet so much alike. It wasn't until the secret was discovered that Harley could see the resemblance in their ways. From the little he knew of Howard's past, he sensed a great deal of emotional and physical suffering at the hands of Kingsley Spencer. His life before that had never been a topic of conversation.

"Are you about finished with the dishes, Howard?"

"Soon Boss. Oh, I guess I need to call you brother now, huh?"

"About that, Howard, can we go out on the porch and have a brotherly chat?"

"Let's go. The rest of the kitchen can wait."

Once seated on the white rockers, Harley indicated by a motion of his head that he would listen as Howard relived his life before the Inn. Trying to conceal his mixed emotions with a sarcastic tone, his words seemed worn and empty. One minute he spoke with bitterness towards his mother and minutes later, a gentleness could be heard in his voice. He broke down as visions of his toy trucks came to mind and a dark- haired woman with no face. As hard as he had been trying, he could not draw out any memories of his mother's appearance. In the past, his thoughts of her were dark, but reading her letter to Freedom's mom sanctioned some light on his previous judgement. He no longer blamed her for abandoning him.

Harley sat quietly as he listened to the saga of his brother's life. He could see the invisible wall Howard spent so many years building and defending, shatter right in front of his eyes. The realization he was still crippled by the fact he had always considered himself written off as a man without a future, because he was a man without a past, came as a shock.

Filled with embarrassed discomfort, Howard sought refuge in Harley's presence. "Harley, it's as if the old Howard Douglas never existed. I feel like I've been given a whole new identity. Is that possible?"

"Anything's possible, Howard. Do you know how fortunate you are to receive another try at life? I guess that's one thing we have in common. Not everyone gets a second chance." Harley shook his head in complete understanding, as his advice continued. "You're an inspiration around here, and especially to me. I can't begin to tell you what it means to me to find a blood relative and I'm especially happy that you're male. Having a sister would be nice, but I think you and I, as men, will be able to connect in a special way."

Harley detected some awareness in Howard's attitude of recognizing his newly found convictions but he could also see him shying away from the humiliation all this was causing.

"Howard, I know you're happy about finding family and about finding Freedom. She seems like a good fit for you. Despite your trials and tribulations, you and Freedom have found each other and are overcoming those adversities. You should be proud, not humiliated."

With a hopeful glint in his eyes, Howard looked at Harley and said, "Do you remember when I told you not to preach at me?"

Harley nodded back at him without speaking.

"I still don't want you preachin' at me, but I *am* willing to take your advice." He smiled with an air of pleasure. "Since you are the oldest!"

The two stood and shared a brotherly hug, patting each other on the back.

CHAPTER 40

The heart of man plans his way, but the Lord establishes his steps.

Proverbs 16:9

Adam Draper was now manager of United National Bank and was pleasantly surprised to meet Howard. After all the introductions were made, he invited everyone into his office for some privacy. This was not the kind of news that needed to be on the front page of the local newspaper.

Before diving directly into business, Adam reminisced a bit about Howard's mother, Helen. He condensed her story and spoke fondly of the woman he remembered, who, because of tragedy, could not take care of her son. "She had no known relatives, with the exception of Howard, and she had decided to assign ownership of the bar to her long-lost best friend, Effie Hunter. The contract stipulated that Effie must prove she used all opportunities to find Howard, and if after ten years she was not successful, she would own the bar, fair and square. I tried to discourage her from this transaction but she was adamant. She was savvy with her investment ideas and insisted on several accounts being established with the same rulings. She was a woman who left no stones unturned."

Adam was evidently speaking to everyone in the room but had focused on Howard. "Helen was a broken woman. A broken- hearted woman. When her husband died, it was as if most of her died too and she couldn't recover. I heard her say many times how much she loved you." He continued with much emphasis on his next words. "Sometimes love just isn't enough. She left you all she had. It was all she could do."

Adam rose from his chair and held out his hand, hoping he had helped to restore Helen's legacy. Howard returned the handshake realizing he was once again a rich man, only this wealth was different from his posh days as a casino czar. This richness, marinated in love, had found its way across many miles and wrestled with many obstacles in order to reach him. It was the kind of love he always dreamed about. It was the kind of love he wanted to give Freedom and because of everyone at Summer Rain, he was now able to do that. Little by little, he was understanding what it meant to love someone unconditionally and the black memories that once blistered his soul were slowly collapsing into extinction. He was quickly realizing how good it felt to love and be loved.

Abby and Harley drove back to the inn while Howard and Freedom found their way to their new project. Every time they pulled up to the curb, the building looked more intimidating. Discussion with Abby and Harley brought them to a conclusion for its future. In memory of Abby's late husband, Jeff, the brick building was going to be transformed into a rehabilitation center for disabled and homeless veterans. Howard's mother had requested it be a benefit to the community and what better purpose could there be than to support those men and women who fought for our country.

A local architect was hired to renovate the interior using Warren Wright as a consultant. Warren's familiarity with soldiers and their needs was helpful when crafting customized kitchens and bathrooms, to accommodate wheelchairs. The entire building inside was painted soft, warm colors, hoping to deter depression from its inhabitants.

Freedom requested the garden be redesigned and modified into raised beds so that, if needed, could be managed from a wheelchair. Being such an historical part of the building, the bar would remain, but would now only serve non-alcoholic beverages.

They enhanced the original carving of 'The Cave' on the wooden door which led into the mountain and added a plaque with a brief description relating to the runaway slaves. The old oak tables, now free of dust, sat ready for some board competition and rowdy card games.

Howard and Freedom waited on the sidewalk for Abby and Harley so they could all walk in together, for the first time since completion.

Warren and Lilly were waiting inside the door, hoping for a powerful reaction, but it was more intense than they expected. There was absolute silence, followed by tears.

Abby was the first to speak. "It's beautiful! Jeff would be so proud. He loved being a philanthropist. His heart would be overflowing with pride right now knowing this charitable organization is proudly displaying his name on the marquis out front." Excitement throbbed in her voice as she celebrated 'The Jeff Weaver Ranch.' "Why are we calling it a ranch?"

Both Howard and Freedom grinned in amusement and said "Follow us." When Abby walked out the back door she was flabbergasted. There, in what used to be a parking lot and several buildings, a stable was erected and six beautiful horses were grazing in the surrounding pasture. Feeling faint, she leaned against the fence for support. "I don't understand how this all happened?"

Still not used to feeling emotions, Howard managed to answer compassionately, "Why do you think we wanted you to wait until the entire project was finished? We found out that Jeff was a true believer in using horses as part of PTSD therapy. We still have room for a few other animals later on. Also, each resident may have a service dog, if they want. We wanted to surprise you with the stables."

Harley spoke up next, all the while, studying the face of the woman he loved. He began talking with wide sweeps of his arms, "This all is in memory of Jeff and Shirley. None of this would have come to fruition without them. I only wish Shirley could be here to help honor Jeff. She was the link that brought us all together."

Abby, still in disbelief, asked how they could possibly afford all of this.

Howard beamed as he excitedly answered her question, "When the town council heard about our project, they notified the Veterans Administration and requested grants to help complete our vision. Isn't it wonderful to know our government is so willing to support our troops? They came through with enough funding to allow more than just the living quarters we had planned."

Abby smiled, out of an overflow of happiness. She could almost hear Jeff and Shirley's undiluted laughter as they gave each other a high-five.

CHAPTER 41

You are the God who works wonders; you have made known your might among the peoples.

Psalm 77:14

Between Summer Rain and the Weaver Ranch, Freedom and Howard were so busy they had no time to concentrate on themselves. The farm was still in need of some repairs but the major renovations were finished and now it was just a matter of maintenance. Word-of-mouth brought more applicants to the rehab center than there were rooms or nurses and the waiting list grew larger every day. Howard watched Freedom as she arranged and rearranged schedules so that a nurse would always be on duty. She seemed to have a knack with paper work. She worked miracles with authorities when needing building permits and she had an uncanny way of finding loop holes in the system. By the time the project was done, no one in City Hall wanted to question Freedom.

Howard had enough money to buy any size diamond he wanted for Freedom but he knew she would want a ring that attracted no attention. He found the perfect solitaire for her and carried it around in his pocket for weeks. He couldn't seem to find the right time to pop the question. But he was going to do it soon.

Freedom just made her last cup of tea for the evening and curled up on the couch when Howard walked in. He seemed really nervous and she thought something must have happened with his dinner at the Inn.

"What's wrong, Howard? You look a bit uncomfortable."

"You got that right my Dear, I've never asked anyone to marry me before and I am a bit anxious."

Freedom's eyes blinked with surprise as her mouth eased into a smile she couldn't control. "Did you say what I thought you just said?"

Howard sank to one knee and repeated the question. "Freedom Hunter, would you do me the honor of being my wife?"

She leaned lightly into him, tilted her face toward his and simply said, "Yes. Yes, I will marry you. When?"

Howard threw back his head and laughed. "That sounds like you're a bit excited? I truly wasn't sure what you would say."

Irritation showed in her eyes as she spoke, "You really didn't know I would say yes? Why would you think that?"

"I love you, Freedom, and I know you love me but I was worried about the word, marry. We've never really talked about commitment." He shrugged matter-of-factly. "I've told you how committed I was to Kingsley but then I ran away from him. I'm sure you'll remember that scenario and wonder if I would do that again, if times get tough."

He rose from his kneeling position and sat next to her on the couch. He clutched her hand and yielded to more emotions than ever before. His eyes filled with tears and the warmth in his expression amazed her. "I never took vows with Kingsley. When I take our vows, I want you to know that I will never violate or disregard the promises we make to each other." His last words were smothered on her lips and the moment his mouth took hers, he felt the invisible threads already binding them, tighten.

Excited to tell Abby and Harley, the newly engaged couple drove to Summer Rain early the next morning. Ecstatic with the news, the women immediately began talking wedding concepts. By the end of the day, the four had embraced the vision of a double wedding.

The very next morning, Abby drove Freedom to the bridal shop. Together they oohed and aahed over the selection of dresses. Abby already determined that she would wear a street length dress in ivory. After all, she had already had a dream wedding and now that she was older she would prefer a more reserved style.

Freedom petitioned Abby's heart to consent to a shared venue – obviously meaning the gazebo. Abby had jotted down ideas about her wedding to Harley ever since the day he proposed and she knew exactly what she wanted to do for the ceremony. Seeing the anxiety building in Freedom, she was willing to adjust. If that meant sharing her day, then that's exactly what she would do and she was sure Harley would feel the same way. She'd seen his face that day, at 'The Cave,' when he realized Howard was his brother. Humble gratitude saturated his character, more so than ever before, releasing long- overdue waterworks. He was embarrassed to be so vulnerable but it had given him a chance to evolve the situation into a spiritual mood.

Harley began by reminding them about the plan God has for all of us. He was given away by his mother to a family who took him to church and the character God instilled in him paved his way to becoming a pastor. His two-year dismissal by the Morning Sun Church provided him with more time to study the Bible, giving him a broader understanding of the importance of perseverance in his life, allowing his allegiance to become stronger to God. He quit fretting about the injustice and simply waited for the Lord's decision. If he had been impatient, the next chapters of his life wouldn't have happened. He believed God led him to Summer Rain and because of Shirley and Abby's trust in him, he was proven innocent and reunited with his congregation.

Harley also expounded on Howard's search. "Meeting Freedom was not a coincidence. I believe God made sure Freedom went to the library that day and he put curiosity in Howard's thoughts so that he would seek her out. It was His plan all along for Howard to be delivered from immoral acts and into a better life. I believe the entire scenario embodies the power of God." He continued with sincerity, "May I remind everyone how walking on a winding road will eventually bring you to a crossroads and that is where you must make a decision. Many times, I have stumbled, not knowing how long the road would be, but always trying to hold on to my faith. Every day I have to ask God to walk beside me." He repeated one of his reflections: "If all of us here wouldn't have gone through our past trials, none of us would be standing here today with each other."

Abby felt so fortunate to have Harley in her daily life and to know he was so willing to help his brother establish better habits. She still was in awe of the recent phenomena that had occurred between Harley and Howard. No one but the Almighty could have intertwined so many people for so many years and then join everyone together at just the right moment. There were times in her life when she hadn't wanted to continue living but now she was glad to be part of a purpose here on earth. She now recognized how God had used her to play an intricate part in two brothers being reunited. An emotional smile alleviated some tension and allowed her body to relax. Thankful for the opportunity to have been shown a miracle, it added another touch of depth to her faith.

CHAPTER 42

A person finds joy in giving an apt reply—
and how good is a timely word!

Proverbs 15:23

Final decisions for both dresses were determined and Abby's street length, lace chiffon wedding dress with an illusion neckline, seemed to be a perfect choice. It was exactly as she had envisioned. Freedom's gown was also the perfect fit for her. The few beaded ruffles, the lace bodice and the long flowing train, provided just enough fancy to satisfy Freedom's wishes, yet implement her 'simple' rule. She was still adjusting to the idea of having store-bought clothes. Picking out a wedding dress was something she never even dreamed about. She was so thankful for Abby's advice.

Harley came around the corner just in time to see the two women in the middle of the gazebo. Freedom was sitting with her sneakers angled on the floor like frogs' feet and Abby was sitting on the built-in bench. They were smiling, but the conversation seemed rather serious.

"Hello ladies. Is this for women only or am I allowed in?"

With a graceful toss of her head, Abby motioned him to come up the steps. "We're trying to make the final decisions for lights and flowers."

Harley was so excited about his secret he could barely hold it together. "Would you two please take a short ride with me?"

"Sorry, Harley, but we really don't have time. We are on a schedule and we can't deviate from it."

Harley deliberately exaggerated the pain in his face and pretended to cry. "Okay, okay, what do you want to show us?"

As they drove down the dirt lane, Abby kept demanding answers until her eyes beheld the most beautiful sight she had ever seen. There before her, was the small stream of rippling water, just as she remembered it. The bank was now lush with leafy plants and wildflowers. The small river rocks were smooth and sparkly, looking like they were scrubbed and polished. A turtle was sunning himself on the newly-created beach. A blue heron stood motionless in the deeper water, obviously waiting for dinner.

Abby's tears fell faster than the miniature water falls. In the midst of so much excitement the last few months, she forgot about hurdling ideas for a retreat toward Harley. "When did you do this?"

"I think if I could have removed the mountain, you wouldn't have noticed. You have been quite busy lately. I hope I have captured a hint of what you want. I thought it would be a great place for the wedding."

Freedom, as foreign as it felt to cry, felt tears running down her checks. "I've never seen anything so splendid."

Distinct shafts of light came bursting through the branches of the Loblolly pines, causing an ambiance of inspiration, giving Abby's vision even more potential. She tipped her face to the sun and shouted, "Did you see that Harley? I think God just gave us his stamp of approval." With an impromptu movement, Abby turned and faced Freedom. "I want to get married here. How about you?"

There was no hesitation in the answer from the aspiring bride. "Yes!"

Abby, wanting to put all the pieces together, was getting ready to ask a question when Harley stopped her." Believe it or not, I think I know what you are going to ask." He winked and without missing a beat, continued with his solution. "I'm sure there is an old hay wagon in Freedom's barn that we could use to transport our guests from the main house to this little corner of our world. We'll decorate the wagon and have it drawn by horses."

Abby's smile saturated the air and that reaction was everything Harley had hoped for. It was truly a smile that reached clear to his heart.

Strong and confident he asked, "Did that answer your concern?"

Peace and happiness shivered through her senses as she whispered, "I guess you do know me, after all."

CHAPTER 43

What therefore God has joined together, let not man separate.

Mark 10:9

The bay colored Clydesdales pranced, performing their traditional march as they pulled the rose covered wagon, filled with guests, to the wedding site. The ride through the woods was beautiful, but nothing compared to the final destination.

Harley had somehow found a way to turn an ordinary grove of trees into a breathtakingly beautiful setting. The first feature the guests saw as they came around the last bend, was the gazebo. It was a bit different than the one back at the Inn, but just as dramatic. Everyone's sense of smell seemed to come alive as they stopped in front of the lattice work, covered in red and white climbing roses.

The seating was arranged so that everyone could hear and see the crystal-clear water as it trickled over the sparkly rocks. The harpist was playing a modern version of the traditional wedding march as the coachman steered the horses one last time down the lane, announcing the arrival of the two brides, who looked as if they just stepped out of a magazine. Harley and Howard were both taken aback by their beauty as they helped them step down from the horse-drawn carriage.

As the two couples walked up the white paper walkway, the pastor was waiting for them, ready to join them together as husband and wife. A lady from Harley's congregation began singing the traditional wedding ballad, "There is Love," causing tears to flow freely.

Harley couldn't take his eyes off Abby during the entire song and he could no longer deny the evidence that Abby truly did love him. She was standing here in front of him, their family and friends, ready to commit her life to him. It was more than he ever dreamed possible. He glanced at Howard and by the expression on his brother's face, he could tell he was feeling the exact same way. Freedom unlocked Howard's heart and soul just as Abby helped to untie the strings that bound him to society's scorn.

Abby's heart was fluttering wildly in her breast as Harley declared his vows to her. He was so handsome in his black tux, her breath caught in her throat. His mouth quivered as he affirmed his love for her, speaking with his own charming expressions only he could do.

Carried away by her own response, she failed to notice her voice had also become fragile as she tried to convey her feelings of happiness and true love for the man standing beside her. She simply spoke from her heart, hoping to reassure Harley one more time about how much she loved and needed him.

Harley was gloriously restored from any brokenness he ever suffered. Abby's words and her obvious commitment to him reinstated any uncertainty that he ever felt.

Howard seemed mesmerized with his brother's vows until Freedom began declaring her love for him. He almost stopped breathing. She was saying things about him that no one had ever said before. Things like how kind he was and how he charmed his way into her life, bringing light into her dark world.

Howard suddenly lost his power of speech. His eyes were clinging to Freedom's, analyzing what he just heard. Harley nudged his brother, hoping to rouse him from his trance. Howard got the hint and began his practiced speech; only it didn't sound like it had in front of the mirror. He heard his voice vibrating with feeling, something he was going to have to get used to. He concluded his wedding vows and leaned over as he kissed the salty tears from Freedom's cheeks.

The pastor pronounced the two couples husband and wife and introduced them to their guests.

Back at the inn, the caterers were waiting with food-laden tables. The band was playing popular Beatle tunes. The photographer was waiting by the gazebo, hoping for some snapshots of the newlyweds. Not waiting for an announcement, Harley and Howard grabbed their wives' hands and led them to the center of the red carpet, laid out as a dance floor. Everyone stood in silence as they witnessed a most tender love scene between the newlyweds as they danced to the Carpenter's "We've Only Just Begun".

No one wanted the evening to end, but the musicians were packing up their equipment and the food servers were placing left over food in containers to be carried into the house. The guests were slowly departing from the celebration, congratulating each couple and wishing them many years of happiness.

Lilly and Warren were the last to leave and as Lilly gave Abby a goodbye hug, she whispered, "I'm pregnant". Abby laughed in sheer joy. She knew Lilly and Warren's life would now be complete. "I am so happy for the two of you." She turned toward Harley and announced, "Honey, we're going to be aunt and uncle!"

Harley gave Warren a big slap on the back, shook his hand and said, "It couldn't happen to a more deserving couple. Congratulations!"

Technically, Howard and Freedom had met at the library but the farm played an important role in their love story, sanctioning their devotion to each other. They left the Inn, anxious to begin their life as husband and wife, allocating the farm as an endless melding of each other. They would begin their honeymoon in their own little sanctuary.

Harley and Abby held each other's hand as they turned out the lights from the celebration and walked into the house that gave them refuge from the outside world.